DRAMA DOLLS

Jason Tanamor

"Drama is life with the dull bits cut out." - Alfred Hitchcock

All Rights Reserved. Copyright © 2019 Jason Tanamor

No part of this book may be reproduced or transmitted in any form or by any means, including photocopying, recording, or by any information storage and retrieval system, without permission in writing from the copyright owner.

This is a work of fiction. Names, characters, places and incidents of the story either are the product of the author's imagination or are used fictitiously, and any resemblance to any actual persons, living or dead, events or locales is entirely coincidental.

This book was printed in the United States.

Visit Jason Tanamor on the web at www.tanamor.com.

ISBN/SKU: 9780578512884
ISBN-Complete: 978-0-578-51288-4

First Edition: May 2019

10 9 8 7 6 5 4 3 2 1

Drama Dolls

A novel by Jason Tanamor

ALSO BY JASON TANAMOR

Adult/Literary:

Anonymous

Humor:

Hello Fabulous!
She's the One?

"Tanamor writes like a deformed love child of Chuck Palahniuk and Charles Bukowski who has finally discovered its own voice..." – Publishers Weekly

Sunday:

JUMPING IN A CIRCLE NEARLY caused her ankle to turn. Heel slipping off the bed, her thigh flexing to maintain position, Brittney's body leaned forward to avoid falling onto the floor. Standing upright helped prevent the near drop off the king sized bed. It was a balancing act.

Avoiding the fall, the jumping commenced.

In the air, the duo aimed higher and higher with every leap. Their knees bending to ensure maximum height. Calves flexing for greater power. Spinning round and round, Brittney's hands locked onto Barb's wrists.

A frozen expression on Barb's face, her eyes big and round. Her skin the color of peach. Makeup immaculate. Perfume was sprayed all over. Apricot and ginger in the air; it was a citrus aroma.

Their heads were so close to the ceiling they could see spider webs. There was paint in and out of a straight line where the wall met the ceiling. White spots along the border. At that height, Brittney could see the trim needed an extra coat.

The room below was a disaster area.

Pained from continual bouncing, the paleness of Brittney's ankle turned to purple. The spinning became tougher, stiffer, with every jump. Her foot had gradually wound itself into the blankets. Twisted into a knot, the fabric suffocated her leg, a temporary relief for the discomfort that was swelling before her.

The knot forced Brittney and Barb to stop and untangle.

Hiking up her knee until her foot dislodged from the comforter, Brittney's heartbeat decreased.

The momentum was disrupted.

Jumping on a bed didn't seem nearly as fun as it had when Brittney and Barb had first entered the home. The up and down motion died to a complete halt. The springs in the mattress rebounded. The two bed jumpers stopped all action.

Play time was over. Now, they had to work. Then they had to escape.

Drama Dolls

Butted up against the wall was a vanity. The reflection in the vanity mirror summed up the prior evening's agenda. The plan that had been schemed up at Brittney's house once again became a reality. Drawers were pulled halfway out, clothes dumped onto the floor. Some articles hanging by their sleeves, stretched from the drawer knob to the wood surface.

Their own reflections, the veracity was staring them in the face.

Picture frames were tilted over. Stock photos from retail stores showed prices and smiling couples, all in black and white. None of the frames were personalized. In the mix, there were different sized frames - 5X7, 8X10, 4X6 – with similar designs. You could tell they were bought in a pack.

The room's plants were dying from lack of water. Leaves crumbling to the floor, the dead ones were a yellowish brown. The plant's soil was dry like dirt. Plant soil dried on the inside of the pots.

A near-full bottle of antidepressants sat alone on an end table, the child safety cap still intact. Information sticker peeled off around the top. The bottom was partially showing – the medication's refill amount and prescription number.

On the dresser was a dust blanket with a clear

spot in the middle that was the shape of a television base. The television had been elbowed to the floor. Surrounding the spot were candelabras with unused candles. Perfectly cylindrical without a hint of melted wax.

The DVD player shoved back into the paint made a dimple in the drywall. Movies in and out of cases splayed like a deck of cards. Romantic comedies. Dramas. Old Bing Crosby movies, black and white; the classics. Widescreen special editions, remastered for maximum viewing. Musicals lined up together, tipping over and sliding down to the surface.

Murder mystery novels stacked as high as a shoe box. Many of the paperbacks with bookmarks in random pages. Romance fiction alphabetized by last name. There were soft-core female porn books. The pages worn and curled at the ends. The cover designs were all the same sequence involving a muscular Adonis with long, flowing hair.

Looking in the mirror, Brittney caught Barb's reflection. She looked like a child trick-or-treating. Holding her bag up for goodies. Standing in the center of the mess, searching for something else to grab. Kneeling down to pick up a watch, Barb kicked away some socks hoping to uncover more treasure. Only seeing wood floor, the burglar dropped the watch in the bag.

Drama Dolls

Toed out from under the bed, a Pink Lady Fleshlight with its cap missing rolled up next to a reserve of porno flicks. In the stash were unconventional, classic movies such as *Alice in Wonderland, Anna Obsessed, Behind the Green Door,* and *China Sisters.*

The sex toy's rubber vagina, it was torn at the lips and scuffed. The bottom part of the labia sticking together. There were fingerprints running up and down the black, dirty handle. The smell of dried milky rubber filtered into the warm air.

Watching the scene unfolding through the mirror made Brittney nauseous. Trying to read the book titles made her dizzy. She began to get lightheaded. The little voice inside, soft and baritone, it was supposed to steer Brittney in the right direction. It was supposed to watch over her. Prevent her from making life mistakes. Instead, the voice, it was rooting Brittney on.

The pillowcases filled to the brim; their tops were crimped closed. Sagging at the bottom, the weight was getting heavier and heavier. Indents at the bottom of the sacks, some round; others pointed. The objects that had sharp edges made black creases on the outer fabric of the pillowcases.

A wooden wardrobe tipped over, petite sized shirts half hanging out, the rest of the garments were scattered on the floor. There were hair ties behind the cabinet; dust bunnies in bunches. Used condom wrappers that had fallen down to the hardwood. The bedroom had dirt and paint chips peppered along the room's perimeter. Dead spiders on their backs, their legs were a cocoon around their bodies. Flies trapped in corner webs. You could tell the room hadn't been cleaned in a while.

A maze of unwanted costume jewelry with no clear paths surrounded the bed. The lamp falling off an end table, hanging from its cord, it was a bungee jumper off a bridge waiting to be retrieved. The shade was rolling back and forth in a circle.

Getting away from the mirror, Brittney's vision refocused.

In the closet was a thick cardboard box the shape of a rectangle. Taped to the top of the box was an empty plastic sleeve used to hold packing slips. *A flat screen television box? A body pillow?* Moving toward the object, the price tag of $4,999 jumped out at Brittney. She opened the box to find nothing but packing material. A plastic bubble as long as the container. Shrink wrapped items tucked underneath. A cotton bag, a wig, and scented powder. The clean whiteness under her gloves showed dirty fingerprints.

Crouching over the fallen cabinet, searching for missed valuables, Barb said, "What do you got there?" As

Drama Dolls

she inquired, she began pulling out pieces from the wardrobe. Rolled socks and stockings in her hand. Dropping them as she looked at her partner.

Stepping out of the closet, empty handed, Brittney shrugged. "No idea." Wiping off her fingertips on a shirt on the floor, shaking her head, she said, "I have no fucking clue."

An untouched display hand on the vanity, made from black velour with a styrofoam base, the annulary, or third finger, was covered with a single diamond ring. The rest of the hand bare, the display hand's wrist was mutant long, nearly a foot in inches, to accommodate bracelets. The 18k yellow gold, round solitaire in a cathedral setting caught Brittney's attention. Reaching for it, she flinched when something crept up behind her.

Headlights shined through the room. The criminals stopped in mid-action, looked out over the yard, through the tree branches. The leaves made it problematic to see. Their shadows moving across the walls and onto the ceiling as the passing car receded down the block. The way the lights entered the house made for an uneventful light show.

Their burglary target was off a public drive with a handful of houses. Bus stop signs were on each corner. Benches by the signs surrounded by half-filled soda cups from fast food joints across town. An outline of a Colonel. Golden arches. Plain white cups from convenience stores. People walking dogs forced to stop as Tiger the collie or Bailey the beagle sipped flat black cola.

The neighborhood was rebuilding. Some houses chipped with paint, others spoiled with Superman yellow or a fresh gray coat with burgundy trim. There was a rental property with multiple cars in the drive. Hanging up outside the unit, there were tin mailboxes in a row counting up to four. The reflective numbers peeling at the edges. Basketballs were on the lawn. One flat, its shape like a bicycle helmet.

Other dwellings, single-family homes with Big Wheels and bicycles on the porch. Hammocks and rocking chairs, a hit during this time of the year. Shade perennials in pots lined up in a row. Mats that read WELCOME were crookedly positioned on the porches.

Wind chimes hanging from porch ceiling hooks, ringing as the breeze brushed through them.

The car light's glow dissipating, Brittney's attention turned to Barb, who was now stepping over the closet to un-trap herself. Footprints made from clean, white cheerleader shoes were stamped into lingerie, evening gowns, and lacy stockings.

Barb's pillowcase was thrown over her shoulder.

Drama Dolls

Bags in her grasp, her pom-poms stuffed into her Spankies. Rubber bracelets around each wrist spread positive words. BELIEVE. BE CONFIDENT.

Hands filled with goodies, Barb was a successful trick or treater, hauling away the most treats.

Her hair made from Saran and Kanekalon, Barb looked flawless. Of all the choices, she'd settled on a mixed hairstyle of artificial fibers. The Midwest weather required the Drama Dolls to combat the sunlight and humidity while resisting the heat so that their hairdos would remain in place. For the most part, their hair stayed styled.

Heavier in material, Saran repelled damage.

Softer to style, Kanekalon fought temperature.

Mid-summer brought insects and humidity. The season also saw children at soccer practice until the sun set. Parents chatting after practice. They were setting up play dates and book clubs. Adolescents running rampant from the extra time off school. Running around until the street lights illuminated the roads. Residents mowing their lawns last minute as the darkness approached.

Brittney's inner voice, it was bitter toward the residents whose lives were fulfilled. Whose lives were happy. Possibly the reason it wasn't deterring the burglary addiction.

The longer days meant late-night break-ins; often times the dates on the calendar changed. Burglaries into the early hours. Waiting for the final light on the block to go black. Sorting goods until the sun came up.

Staring at Barb, Brittney stood statue-still. Her plastic face lifted from the wide smile stretched across the mask. Her phony eyes were fully expanded.

"What?" Barb said unfazed, her red cherry lipstick, thicker than the border's paint. The black dot in the center of her pearl colored mouth was miniscule. Her mannered mouth, unmoved. The mask made the words muffled at times. Talking with your lips rubbing plastic, it was a challenge. She said, "What're you looking at?"

Taken aback, emotions running high, the voice inside an innocent schoolgirl, Brittney said, "You look beautiful. Totally beautiful."

Cheeks stained pink, her eyebrows the shape of moons, Barb's bulged eyes displayed no emotion. The false eyelashes fanned outward. They were evenly spread out.

The Doll's hair fell down the sides of her thermoplastic polymer face. Brushed straight but slowly expanding from the humidity coming from the open windows.

Eye holes the size of an infant child's coat button made the housebreaks difficult. Talking through a plastic

Drama Dolls

mouth that didn't move made for miscommunication. The fake breasts mounted on their chests, they made for impure thoughts. Constructed from cardboard, each breast was shaped like a computer mouse. Now and then, the staple poked their skin, the clear tape scratching their chests. The Dolls' "boobs" were snug and tight from the bras that they wore. Safe and sound under the tight turtleneck cheerleader sweaters.

The minor annoyances, though, were worth the price to be seamless. They were worth the price to be cheerleaders. Worth the price to be Drama Dolls.

Reaching out, Barb Doll flipped the loose strands of hair away from Brittney's face. Breathing heavier, through the mask, she said, "You're totally beautiful." An awkward stare, she moved in toward Brittney, their open mouths touching. Their bodies rubbing, the sharp cardboard edges of Brittney's breasts scratched her chest. She could feel a staple twisting. It was poking her nipple.

The voice inside, it was hooting and hollering.

Pulling back, Brittney said, "Totally!" Underneath the plastic, her real smile was wide. Wider than the manufactured mouth on the mask. All things considered, Brittney's life was currently happy. It was content.

"Ready?" Barb said.

"Ready."

Barb, flicking her head toward the bedroom door, said, "Let's move."

Running out of the house, breaking toward the darkness down the street, Barb slung around a pillowcase and hiked up her mini-skirt.

Her legs were toned and tanned, thigh muscles working on each step. Her calves flexed into the shape of biscuits when each foot hit the pavement. Running with bags of loot made for complete awkwardness in her stride.

Looped around her wrists, the remaining bags rammed into Barb's legs, bruising spots that would later turn yellow. The pom-poms' handles poked her belly, the plastic feathers tickling her upper thighs.

Passing through a used car lot, the Kia models and Hondas lined up in a row. A pair of minivans with slashed prices parked side by side. The scrolling marquee of a sign read NO CAR OVER $6,995. Financing was available with approved credit. The marquee, it read the days and hours of operation.

Catching her reflection in each car window she passed, Brittney stopped periodically to stare. Her transparent image doubled in with each automobile's interior.

Slowing to a walk, Brittney spotted a vintage Corvette in the corner of the lot. It had a sign that read

Drama Dolls

PRICE BREAK. Looking through the reflection, into the custom bucket seats, Brittney imagined cruising around town in flair. Turning heads, people pointing as the car rolled by.

The voice, it was screaming, "Buy it!"

Barb, gaining distance, turned around and jogged backward. She said, "C'mon!"

Catching one last glimpse at coolness, Brittney Doll picked up the pace and rejoined her fellow cheerleader.

The plastic Dolls passed a law office on the corner of an intersection; the sign on the building was for customers only. The red brick building stood out amongst the old fashioned neighborhood they were running through.

Once they got back onto the street, the Drama Dolls sprinted toward freedom.

The more pressure on her ankle, the more Brittney began to limp. She was running with the bulk of the weight to one side. Losing pace, slowing down to a gallop.

"OK?"

Shifting the possessions to her weak side to even out the weight, Brittney nodded. Looking back toward the house, through the little black squares for windows, the aftermath shined periodically as cars drove past. A rolling shadow on the ceiling the shape of a hand, one finger thicker below the knuckle.

Continuing down the street, weaving in and out of yard bushes, ducking at cars that passed by, the fleeing burglars managed the escape as planned. Walking farther away from civilization, through a wooded area, the stream water dripping on the rocks, the Drama Dolls had struck again.

The leaves rustled under their feet as the two trudged down the path that separated hills and water. Bags slung around their shoulders, Brittney and Barb slowly caught their breaths.

Far enough out, past the woods and multi-lane street that connected the neighborhood and downtown area, the pair ducked into an alley and removed their plastic masks. Breaths exhaled, the night's heat causing them to sweat. A stench of rotten food and stale urine punched them in the face.

Brittney and Barb looked at each other and cringed.

The alley served as a dumpster spot for various restaurants. Sesame chicken leftovers in one dumpster. Mixed in were peanuts and chili peppers from discarded Kung Pao splattered over rice. The smell of soy sauce

Drama Dolls

lingering.

Fried chicken dumped out in another. Bones with skin and fat rolled into napkins. Cardboard buckets with grease spots on the bottom were tossed in as well. Layered in on top of the chicken were refried beans from the taco joint next door. Thrown out ground taco beef, shreds of lettuce, and diced tomatoes splashed on the inside of the bins. Stale taco shells broken into pieces peppered over the pounds of wasted food. The aroma emanating from the dumpster was a smorgasbord.

A couple of Chinese cooks were standing around a dumpster smoking cigarettes. Speaking in their native language, the two were laughing as they inhaled their smokes. "Yào hē zuì jīn wǎn (Going to get drunk tonight)," one cook said to the other. He inhaled his smoke, and then exhaled a couple of charcoal gray colored donuts into the air.

The other cook, spitting into the pavement, said, "Bù, yào ná qǐ háizi (Nah, have to pick up the kid)."

The drinking cook, hoping to get an entire twelve pack into his system before night's end, said, "Tài zāogāole, yěxǔ míngtiān (Too bad, maybe tomorrow)."

The child touting cook, he smiled, nodded his head, and then flicked his cigarette butt into the distance. Waiting for his co-worker to finish his smoke, he kicked a couple rocks away from him. Once his friend was finished, the two Chinese men entered the back door of the restaurant, disappearing from view.

Excess hamburgers were piled to the top of the remaining garbage can. The bums were stocking up for the week. Mice scurried from under the dumpsters. Birds were drinking from puddles formed by water dumped out from kitchens. There was piss splattered where the buildings met the pavement.

Swallowing hard, Brittney said, "Yuck!"

"Totally," Barb said. A bird flew by with half a bun in its beak. It dropped a crumb that landed on Barb. "Not cool!" she said, wiggling her arm. The piece of food fell down to the pavement. A mouse ran up to the bread and snatched it, running away before Barb could know what happened.

The heist had gone well, a treasure of materialistic belongings for their stash.

"Drama Dolls Strike Again!" the inner voice of conquering reason said.

Barb locked gaze with Brittney, their hearts beating heavy. Gasping for air, they nodded, the Dolls' real lips building to smiles. Masks on top of their heads, the plastic faces crumpled, looking up to the stars. Empty eye holes stared into nothing.

Drama Dolls

"Great work, Barb."

"You too, Brittney."

Crumbling gravel in the distance startled them. Nodding their heads sharply down, each mask slipped to the respective cheerleader's chin. The getaway car, a black Buick LeSabre boat, crept around the corner, its headlights turned off. It was purring through the night. The large body fit just enough in the alley for the car's doors to open.

In the backseat were bags filled with necklaces, bracelets, loop earrings, and stud earrings. The bags had tiaras, rings, and chokers. A Pearl Drop Tattoo choker was sticking out of the top of one bag. The bits of jewelry, they were the lifted contents the cheerleader Dolls had to sort through later. Prior heists that also went as planned.

Slouching against the door in the backseat was a passed out Drama Doll. Her body, it was limp and hunched down. Her head fallen into the window. Uniform wrinkled, the shirt was scrunched up halfway over her torso so you could see her navel ring. Shaven legs from the knees down; blade cuts were a music staff without notes. Thighs were a smooth satin. The doll wore spotless white shoes. Her right one untied.

The passenger side door swung open. Leaning over into the front passenger seat, Lena screamed, "Get in!" The Doors played softly out of the speakers. Melancholy keyboards complementing the guitar riffs.

Masks positioned, Brittney and Barb tossed the loot into the car. Sliding up against the bags in the backseat, Barb made herself as comfortable as she could. Squeezing in pushed the passed-out Drama Doll's head farther into the window. The mask was looking ghostly through the glass. Staring out toward the direction of the heist, Barb said, "Let's go!"

Birds flew off with hamburger buns. Soaring in front of the car, through the windshield, the cheerleaders could see bread crumbs dropping onto the street. A homeless man digging into a dumpster pulled out a chicken leg. Biting into the meat, his teeth pulled the skin from the bone. The vagrant swallowed his score and then scooped out taco meat with his hand, throwing the chunks into his mouth simultaneously with the dark meat.

Brittney and Lena looked at each other and winced. "Gross," Lena said.

Her own plastic mask over her head, hair pulled back in a ponytail, Lena shifted into drive. Hands were covered in gloves around the steering wheel. On her feet were white cheerleader shoes. Her mini-skirt layered over a pair of runny pantyhose. Lena looked exactly like them — totally beautiful.

Observing the passed out, dolled up freak show, Barb said, "What's with her?" Brittney stayed quiet. Although Lena stayed silent as well, she made a point to stare at Barb through the rearview. The silence in between the music urged Barb to repeat herself. "What's with her?" she said, this time louder.

Speeding away, Lena remained quiet. Jim Morrison singing "Light My Fire." Lena lip syncing Morrison through her mask. Her plastic lips rolling up and down to the words.

"Tired… she's just tired," Brittney said. Looking over at Lena, the air thickening from the discomfort, Brittney quickly changed the subject. Her thumb pointing over the seat, she said, "This is Barb. Barb, this is Lena." Rubbing her ankle with her hand, the heat from the friction started to burn Brittney's leg.

"Yea, we've meh-"

Clearing her throat, Lena cut Barb off. She craned her neck back and gave Barb a sharp, dirty look.

Outside the back car window, the alley was shrinking to the size of a faraway train tunnel. Eying Barb, the darkness hiding her gaze, Lena said, "Hi. Nice to meet you."

Gazing out the window, avoiding Lena's stare, Barb slid down in her seat. "A pleasure."

Of course, Barb's real name was William.

And Brittney's was Jeffrey.

Before the burglaries, William and Jeffrey would dress up as adult cheerleader Dolls in the comfort of their own homes. It wasn't just them, though. There were adult cheerleaders as far as eternity. The beautiful thing about the World Wide Web was you could have a group of peppy cheerers leading rallies in the privacy of their bedrooms. A multitude of one-person pyramids toppling over to the ground. Kicking their legs up and standing like a statue with their arms straight up. The open curtain, open window, was the student body in the stands.

Behind the monitor screens, the Dolls simultaneously typed into the little chat box at the bottom of the website. Many of them shared stories throughout the day.

An online group for fetishes, William slowly blasted out emails to build his community - a community of adult Dolls who shared his passion for being beautiful. For being accepted.

William, he grew up obese and his skin was full of acne. His teeth were a row of baked beans. Pushed down

Drama Dolls

into the dirt the beans were either straight or crooked, leaning toward the left of his face. Much of his childhood had been riddled with bad fortune. His self-esteem never blossoming.

Sitting on a playground bench, observing a girl as she combed the hair of her Barbie doll, William had seen the girl's smile widen like the doll's manufactured lips. Watching the young child hug her doll, kissing it as she held it in tightly, the overweight loner witnessed true happiness. Something he had never himself experienced. Now, he was trying to recruit others.

Jeffrey would gradually log in at random intervals to see the group's posts. Most of the posts came from William. Instead of feeling sorry for himself, Jeffrey felt compassion toward William, who had wanted to be beautiful for so long.

Over time, members dropped out, disappeared, or grew out of the phase. The online community's participation lessened. Posts reduced. There were only a handful of members commenting. Penis enlargement pills and discounted sex toys were the only advertisements being pimped out.

After a while, the membership dwindling, William and Jeffrey took their passion out to the real world. Decked out in full cheerleader outfits, the two visited retail stores, pricing out televisions and computer equipment. They shipped packages via ground through the post office. William and Jeffrey attended rock concerts. Experiencing the reactions from people made them feel important.

Dressing as Drama Dolls, sipping lattes at coffee houses, the stares fed into their sickness.

Eyes burning through their backs, snickering when the two cheerleaders passed by, after a while, the rush began to fade away. The people around them became artificial. As if William and Jeffrey were sitting behind a computer again.

To keep the momentum alive, Jeffrey suggested crimes. Not murders or assaults, nothing of the sort; rather, his plan involved home invasions. Stealing. Looting. For the rush, exhilaration.

This most recent burglary, a dozen's worth of stash collected, was the beginning of the end for Jeffrey. It was the beginning of the end for the Drama Dolls.

The getaway lasted the entire Doors album. "People Are Strange" going into "Break On Through" going into "Love Me Two Times," the entire drive was a fog. The rawness of Robby Krieger's riffs complementing

Drama Dolls

Morrison's vocals took Brittney back to a different time. A different life. A life before she met Her. It took her back to a life before the Drama Dolls.

The depth of Morrison's voice was haunting at this hour. Ray Manzarek tickling the keys brought chills through the plastic coated figure's spine. It didn't help that the night was in full swing, allowing the drive to be pitch black at times.

Brittney looked over at Lena. The driver's attention was fixed on the road ahead of them. The ghostly profiled mask, seemingly glowing in the night, brightened under each street light that the car passed.

Craning her neck into the backseat of the car, Brittney saw Emily slumped down into the seat. The car's wheels rolling over bumps on the road caused the passed out doll's neck to swivel. At times, her limp head bobbled as the Buick rolled into divots in the street. The movement of Emily's neck accompanied Morrison's voice as it echoed throughout the speakers. As if she was singing along.

Mixing in with passing intersections, parked cars, fire hydrants, and sidewalk cracks was Emily's faint cheerleader face coming into focus through the car window's reflection. The frightening image, coupled with the claustrophobia of the mask crowding Brittney's face, her nostrils encumbered by thermoplastic polymer, caused her to fall in and out of a stupor.

The Doors had entered Jeffrey's life when high school graduation was within grasp. A group of friends, one whose father worked the graveyard shift, together they would hang out in Paul's basement, drinking Milwaukee's Best. Listening to his older brother's music. Queen, Steve Miller, the Doors, they all were on constant rotation.

Paul's mother lived in another state; a recent divorce resulting in Paul learning to "deal" with it.

Passing the time, the friends tossed empty aluminum cans into a pile. Miller singing "The Joker," the late night chill sessions started with their core group of buddies. Poker hands dealt - seven card stud, five card draw - the games helped idle away the hours until it was time to sleep. Until it was time to repeat the cycle.

A half dozen kids avoiding the police in a relaxed state until adulthood.

Gradually, the monotony forced Paul to invite others. Football players, jocks from other lettered sports, high school cheerleaders, hippies, and underclassmen, they all came and went at their leisure. One night could see a

Drama Dolls

dozen folks while other evenings could witness entire classrooms of students.

The basement crowd filtered into the living room, which then made its way into the attic. Students did their laundry when they spilled vodka and other identifiable liquids. There were semen stains that mixed in with cigarette ashes while the spin cycle ran. Random panties and boxer shorts fraternized with Paul's clothes. Loose change, house keys, necklace charms, they all consorted in an ashtray to be collected later. As the parties continued, the lost and found emptied until the ashtray was used for its intended purpose, a dropping point for cigarette butts.

Pizzas were delivered in bulk. The driver becoming familiar with the gatherings, he would stop over after his shift. He became a regular, singing along with Freddie Mercury. Dancing along with the Doors. In uniform, jumping up and down while the music blasted, he hit the high notes in key. All the while, his plastic badge was being shuffled around the house. The pizza guy ruled "Fat Bottomed Girls." A background filled with music lessons, the gang soon discovered. Those were the days Jeffrey was "normal." The days before he met Her.

Now, anytime a Doors, or Queen, or Steve Miller song played, the confused and lost boy came out in Jeffrey. The internal dialogue, it said, "Break on through to the other side."

Lena slammed on the brakes. A wild squirrel running across the street. Coming out from her reverie, Brittney shook her head. "Sorry," Lena said.

Fleeing the scene, with Brittney riding shotgun, each block looked the same. Houses in one area were dated back to Victorian times - a historical district. Queen Anne styled homes. Unbalanced facades covered by wraparound porches. Overhanging eaves with decorative support brackets. There were dentils around the roof outlines on a number of the houses. The Victorian homes, they had front-facing gables. Their towers, shaped like polygons.

Terraces made of brick, roofs from slate.

The Queen Anne houses were surrounded by brick roads. Uneven bricks with different shades. Red, orange, brown, they all mixed together to add class to the community. Driving into the block was driving into another time.

The cheerleaders drove by a pink, purple, and green-colored painted lady with a square tower as its focal point. The tower was perfectly centered. Behind it toward

Drama Dolls

the back of the house, extending up to the heavens, was a colossal chimney. Wooden shingles to match the trim. The front porch's balustrade was recently painted. One spindle replaced due to wood rot, its color standing out to those walking by.

An open-door event showcasing the homes' interior was peddling donations for the neighborhood's beautification project. "Help keep our neighborhood timeless." There were signs posted in the yards of various houses. White cardboard canvases stapled to stakes in the ground.

Lena pointed to a sign. "We should go to that," she said. In a plastic info tube, hanging from the wooden post, was a stack of flyers promoting the cause. "I would love to see the insides of these houses."

Pulling over to the side of the road, shifting into park, Lena ran out to grab details. Handing the information to Brittney, she drove away. "Read it to me," Lena said, her mouth forming a smile.

Scanning the leaflet, Brittney cleared her throat and offered out the information. "Designed by the same architect, the historic beauties are unique but share similar floorplans," she said. Pulling the paper closer to her face, Brittney said, "Handcrafted plaster outlining the ceiling gives each house an identity. Although the design molded into the plaster is comparable, the custom imprints are often slightly skewed." Where decorative plaster was nonexistent, there was embossed wallpaper covering the ceilings.

Inside the painted ladies, dumbwaiters were for showing off. Many of them were not functional. A few of the dumbwaiters on the block were boarded up, making them a novelty for guests.

The darkness made it difficult to read. Brittney slid her body, holding up the flyer, using the passing streetlights as illumination. "The back staircases, once used for the help, are, today, generally used for shortcuts to the back bedrooms or second routes to the upstairs."

Busy wallpaper, filled with floral patterns primarily colored red or blue, spanned the walls of dining rooms and parlors. The curtains often matched the wallpaper's pattern so that it flowed continually throughout the house. Made from fabric such as velvet or silk, Victorian era homes' window dressings consisted of curtains, cornices, and valances. Holding the curtains back were cords and tassels.

Scanning the document, Brittney said, "The parlors were for entertaining. These rooms are where the family's antique furniture shines. Ornate couches and chairs are a must in this room."

Bedrooms were painted plain colors to

Drama Dolls

complement the quarter's use. Brittney, squinting to read the remaining information, said, "A boy's room would typically be blue and a girl's room would typically be pink."

Barb, screaming over the front seat, said, "How is that any different than today?"

And Lena, excited with the opportunity to expand her tastes, said, "Can we go?"

Turning the flyer over to inspect the back, giving it a once over, Brittney flipped it back around so the information was in front of her. "What's today?" Looking up to the dome light, a calendar forming in her brain, Brittney said, "We missed it. It was today."

Lena's body dropped. Her mouth curled downward. Eyes on the road in front of her, she said, "Poopy."

The Victorian era shrinking behind them, the Drama Dolls approached another neighborhood.

Lena pointed toward a row of Second Empire houses. Derived from architecture during the Second French Empire, the houses dated back to 1865. "Look at that one," Lena said. Barb leaned in between the headrests, propping her elbows up on the bench of a seat, to catch a glimpse.

A steep mansard, or curbed roof, on top of a rectangular tower was as high as the tree in front of it. The tower, centered in the middle of the symmetrical home constructed from red brick, was topped with iron trim. "The brackets under the roof are amazing," Lena said. Releasing her foot off the gas, the getaway car slowing down to a crawl, she said, "I can't believe how ornate they are."

Turning her head to admire the roof, Brittney said, "Corbels. Those are called corbels. They support the cornices of the roof – the ledges." Folding the Victorian flyer in half, Brittney slid the piece of paper in the side door's pocket.

Lena, impressed with Brittney's knowledge of old architecture, counted the corbels as they passed. The speed of the car prohibited her from being successful, the elaborate brackets beginning to run together.

The clear black of the night, the space between each house, broke the monotony of the blurry supports. Next to the brick beauty was an abandoned house waiting to be rehabbed. Chipping at the paint, patches of dry rot needing repair, the empty house had a lot of work ahead.

The Second Empire's roof shingles were falling over themselves. Some were dangling off the edges. Other shingles in the grass in the front of the dwelling. Two of the four columns that supported the porch were off their posts, with sturdy steel beams in their place. The columns,

Drama Dolls

sanded down to their original wood, they were perched up against the house's side.

The front porch was sagging on one end. The joists underneath needing reinforcement. A partial railing constructed, many of the rods were missing or rotted. A ceiling fan hanging from the porch roof appeared to be the only item in working condition.

Furrowing her lips at the eyesore, Lena said, "I bet these houses cost a lot of money to restore." The windows on the second floor were missing shutters; however those inside the porch area were still intact. The shutters still hanging were chipped and rotting.

Barb, she said, "You'd easily dump a couple hundred grand."

Her feet propped up on the dashboard, above the glove compartment, ankle pain receding from not having weight on it, Brittney leaned her head back on the headrest. Her hair was blowing from the air coming in the open window. The warm breeze squirting into the small holes of the mask.

Reaching her hand over toward Brittney, Lena cupped the resting cheerleader's kneecap and began massaging it.

Finishing the block of Second Empires was an asymmetrical mansard on top of a wooden house's left side. The way the house was positioned on the corner closed the block perfectly. A painted beauty, chrome yellow with Venetian red window trim running up and down the exterior, caused Lena to say, "Wow!"

Barb, leaning up to the window to see the entire house, said, "Looks like a Victorian McDonald's."

The inner voice, whispering into Brittney's ear in Victorian slang, said, "I would like fries in my sauce-box."

Turning the corner, Barb's body shifted toward the middle of the car, shoving a bag of jewels into the passed out Drama Doll. "Easy on the turns," Barb said to Lena.

Rotating her head, addressing Barb, Lena said, "Oops."

Barb cut a look to Brittney's propped up legs. Following her stare, Lena quickly released her hand from the kneecap. Hands returning to the wheel, the car rolled through the remaining historic block.

The architectural neighborhoods finished with an aesthetic block of Richardsonian Romanesque style homes. Combining characteristics from French, Spanish, and Italian Romanesque charms, the castle-like mansions, mostly made from stone, were throwbacks to medieval Europe.

"These works of art were named after the

Drama Dolls

architect Henry Hobson Richardson," Brittney said. Her head cocked at an angle, observing the row of houses, she said, "These are the cream of the crop."

Each house, comparable in design, had short, unusually shaped columns, feudal type arches, and cylindrical towers, which were the main focal points. Pointing up toward a Richardsonian success, Brittney said, "The architect was very eccentric. He had an eye for individuality." Various gabled roofs - side gables, front gables, and cross gables - were typical for the houses.

"Incredible," Lena said, the neighborhood passing by in a flash. When they passed a stretch of Victorian houses intermingled with Colonial Revivals, Prairie, Foursquare, and Neo-Gothic type abodes, the Drama Dolls knew they were getting close to their drop off point – Brittney's house.

Wrought iron fences passed by. Their individual posts made Brittney dizzy. Fences on top of retaining walls. The blocks in the wall spanning the house. Cracks in the blocks, they were as long as the wall itself.

Detached garages doubling up as the car drove passed, Brittney's vision became cloudy. Square garage doors zipping by, all the same size, each complemented a house.

The voice of intoxicated reason said, "You are

acting like you're half-rats."

Her eyes closing to a squint, the streetlights shined their laser beam lights into Brittney's pupils as her head began to spin. Everything slowed down, her life going back to the first birthday after losing Her.

A change in venue altered the guest list. No longer at the ritzy country club, invitations went out to those who knew Jeffrey before the wedding. Those he felt comfortable around. Those who genuinely knew him.

Comprised accordingly, the party hosted a few couples, married friends, and those who'd disappeared a half-year into their marriage.

The cake was rerouted to an old stomping ground. A bar and grill, one of many pre-marriage hangouts that had disappeared after the nuptials. A few bartenders recognized the name on the reservation. Anticipation building, stepping into the establishment was like he'd never left at all.

"Jeffrey!"

The back room displayed a sign made from cardboard letters. The words HAPPY BIRTHDAY! intertwining together, the sign was sagging like a

Drama Dolls

hammock. Purchased at a party store, the juvenile decorations made Jeffrey feel youthful.

Jeffrey's body lifted at the familiarity of the bar. When he saw bartenders from his past, his face brightened up. The setup was still how he remembered it. Tube televisions replaced with flat screens were the only noticeable change. The same beer lights hanging overhead, jukebox with antiquated selections, and bar stools fraying at the edges all made him feel comfortable. They made him forget Her momentarily.

Gray on his beard, his face showing more wrinkles, Henry had tended bar his entire adult life. Cartons of cigarette smoke, late night shifts, and buckets of shots had caught up to him. "Thought that could've been you," he said. His face dry, the white powdery skin was cracking around his mouth. Henry said, "Had we been certain, would've gave you a hard time with the decorating."

"Oh yeah," Jeffrey said. "What would it have read?" A man walked up behind him, a five dollar bill in his hand.

Henry, biting on his lip, holding in a smile, said, "Happy birthday, dickhead!" He laughed to himself, his arm reaching out to tap his old friend's shoulder. "We missed you around here." His teeth over his bottom lip,

Henry grabbed a Coors for the man holding out cash.

The customer said, "Keep the change," and then returned to his table of friends.

Nodding, the birthday boy extended for a handshake.

Henry's hairline was receding to the top of his head. Reaching toward Jeffrey, Henry said, "Good to see you again, my friend."

A dark chocolate cake, made by Jeffrey's colleague, displayed a waxy four and zero on top. White numbers outlined in a bright yellow, they stood bold atop the icing. The co-worker, she'd insisted on baking. "Really, it's no big deal," Kelly said. "You have enough on your mind." Careful with her words, showing her front teeth as she paused, she said, "It must be hard to lose a spouse."

An accounting clerk, her job consisted of payroll, accounts payable, and accounts receivable. A rounded woman, single for all of her life. Lived in a studio apartment. She walked to work no matter the temperature. No siblings. Every night she liked to read. Always nice in the office, giving only tidbits of her life as if they were code words to decipher, Kelly was the perfect employee.

Framing the cake with her hands, admiring her work, she said, "This was so easy to make." Her lips squeezed, Kelly bobbed her head. "Yeah," she said.

Drama Dolls

"Really easy to make."

Standing over the empty cafeteria style table, realizing no one was paying attention, Kelly's eyes found the wall. She looked around the joint, slowly nodding her head as she appreciated the sports art hanging above.

In one setting, Mark Twain was photographed shooting billiards. A black and white picture enclosed in a wooden frame, the author was wearing a white suit with black bowtie. His hair was long. A cigar was extending from his mouth. Leaning over the table, the novelist was aiming the cue ball off the canvas.

Another was an autographed football jersey hanging under glass. Its owner was a local high school All-American. The football star during his tenure, he now owned his own insurance agency.

"You used to hang out here?" she said to Jeffrey.

Oblivious, managing the floor, Jeffrey played every angle of guests, standing center in the bar making eye contact, smiling, and saying hello. Guests around him were holding beers and munching on chips. They were engaging themselves in superficial conversation.

Above the shuffleboard table, a pair of scantily dressed women advertised beer. A brunette holding a beer mug. She was wearing a one piece bathing suit over her hourglass figure. The blonde pouring the beer from a pitcher. Dressed in a bikini, her abs revealed a six-pack missing a can. The poster, it publicized the upcoming Chicago Cubs schedule.

Jeffrey's sole responsibility was to be available. After standing still became boring, he made his rounds. Maneuvering around each guest, weaving in and out of conversations, Jeffrey rejoined Kelly. "Oh, there you are," she said. "No, seriously. Water, cocoa powder, flour, baking soda, uh…" Eyebrows lowering, Kelly took a glimpse toward the ceiling. Deep in thought, her head returning back to the cake to jog her memory, she said, "Oh yeah, powder, salt, butter, sugar, eggs, and vanilla extract."

All the while, the inner voice of bitterness was saying, "Why Her? Why couldn't it have been Kelly?"

Married couple friends sympathizing over the death attended over guilt. A couple months removed from dinner parties and social gatherings. And now they were scarce. Strangers. Only appearing at the birthday party because She had invited them.

Attempting to avoid the awkwardness, showing his "friends" that he still cared, Jeffrey said, "A new house? That's wonderful." Feigning intrigue, he said, "Whereabouts?"

Their response, it was going in one ear and out the

Drama Dolls

other. Jeffrey's attention faded quickly.

Others attended to see how he was holding up. A couple was dressed for a classy gathering. The mister, he wore a black suit and tie over a red buttoned down shirt. And the misses, she wore a V-neck Chiffon floor length dress. Their calculated getaway before the cake was served. "I'm sorry, but we must get going." Their excuses, they were pre-planned on the drive.

There were rounds of drinks circulating the room. Guests who were friends with Her disappearing one by one. Using the restroom and then making a quick exit. Excuses to leave were flying out of people's mouths. "The babysitter has to get home," and "I had a long day," and "Well, we better get going."

"Yeah, you better get going!" it said. The voice of defensive reason influencing Jeffrey's life. Protecting him.

Kelly stayed until the cake was served. Then she walked home. No excuse given.

"Jeffrey!"

By the time the cake was half eaten the crowd consisted of old buddies from the bar scene. Huddled around the bar, Henry behind serving drinks, they all were cautious about Jeffrey's life, hearing only pieces of information from the folks who had better places to be. Or excuses to be made.

"I'm sorry to hear that."

"God, that blows."

Shaking his head in disbelief, Henry poured a round on the house for the remaining guests. Topping off the middle-aged pal's glass, the bartender slid the drink back toward Jeffrey.

"It's getting better. Each day is a challenge," Jeffrey said, offering up his life in segments. Avoiding sudden outbursts, dodging eye contact allowed the solemn topic to transition into other subjects. Holding in the emotion, Jeffrey said, "I miss Her every day. But I have to move on. Otherwise, I'll go crazy."

Mocking internally, his brain, it said, "Otherwise I'll go crazy." It said, "Yeah, *you'll* go crazy!"

Sipping from his beer bottle, Michael said, "It's amazing to see you so normal after something like that." Shaking his head, a television commercial distracted him from the conversation. Balding men finding a spray on cure for only one hundred and fifty dollars. Michael chuckled. "Guaranteed or your money back," the advertisement spit out. Watching until it changed over, he held up his drink and said, "Cheers."

The gang crowding around the bar, catching up with their lives-

Drama Dolls

"Jeffrey!" He had recognized the voice but couldn't find the owner. "Jeffrey!" Feeling his shoulder nudged, Jeffrey/Brittney sharply opened her eyes.

An artificial expression, the smell of plastic in the air, Lena said, "You OK?" Concerned, her arm extended out toward Brittney's lap.

Blinking repeatedly, Lena's face was a ghost becoming less translucent. Surrounded by darkness, the whiteness of her thermosoftening plastic skin frightened Brittney. Looking down at Lena's hand, Brittney shook her head. Staring up at Lena's perfect manmade smile, Brittney's vision came into focus. The image was now crystal clear.

"Are you OK?" Lena said again.

Nodding slowly, her throat filled with saliva, Brittney Doll swallowed.

"Are you sure?" Lena said, her face scrunched up as if in pain. Brittney nodded her head again. Assured that Brittney was conscious and alert in the moment, Lena said, "We're here."

Pulling into the driveway, the door sliding up the rails, Lena cut the car's lights and rolled into the garage.

Coasting to a stop, the garage door closed behind them. Parked in the middle of the two car unit, the group sat until the bay was completely dark.

Without an uttered word for nearly an eternity, Barb, sitting in the middle of the backseat with her head encroaching into the front, said, "Ready?"

Lena nodded. "Ready," she said.

"Let's do it."

The Drama Dolls got to work. Stepping out of the car, one by one by one, they pulled out the bags. The only light escaping from the car's interior. A constant beeping from the door being open.

An assembly line setup, Barb removed the pillowcases from the car, handed them off to Lena, and ended with Brittney tossing them into the house. Some were heavier than the others. Lena prepared Brittney when to expect the weightier bags by her body movements.

Escape vehicle not quite as full, the doors were wide open. As the automobile emptied, Brittney knew what was coming next. Slithering around Lena, sliding up behind Barb, who was looking into the backseat, Brittney cleared her throat.

Barb glanced toward the slouching Doll, her curiosity getting to her. Finger extending toward her, moving closer for examination. The sleeping Doll was

Drama Dolls

shadowed from her position in the backseat. There was no movement, breathing or otherwise that Barb could detect. "What—"

Cutting her off, Brittney said, "Let her sleep. She'll be fine out here." Grabbing Barb's arm and pulling it back, the paranoid cheerleader's heartbeat began to increase.

Inside, the voice echoing to remain calm.

Tension building, the two stared at each other. A mystery in Barb's eyes; a secret in Brittney's. Behind them, Lena, she said, "C'mon!"

Lena entered the house with Barb following. Alone in the garage, brightened just slightly, Brittney watched the dead-weighted cheerleader sleep.

"Brittney!"

Cocking her head toward the voice, Brittney stared into the house. After a brief pause, she slowly returned to observe the unconscious doll. Snaking her body into the car, Brittney leaned in for a kiss.

"Are you coming?" Lena screamed from afar.

Entering the living room, Brittney sat on the floor and joined in on what would be the best part of the heists. Barb and Lena emptying the contents, the pillowcases collapsing to the floor. The sounds of the heist were raindrops on roof shingles. Little thumps on the area rug dying to a halt upon impact. Chain links sounding like

45

rolling thunder.

Shaking the bags to ensure all the contents escaped, gems fell everywhere and on everything. The sofa was covered in jewelry. Bracelets were sliding in between the couch cushions. Bouncing under the love seat, stud earrings lost their partners. Some of the backs flew in different directions. A future pinch on Brittney's toe.

Trinkets speckled around the living room. Empty bags stashed in the corner behind the radiators. The room was the dumping ground for the burglaries. Sitting in a triangle, their bodies equidistant, the bulk of the jewels gathered in the center, the Drama Dolls began sorting through the contents confiscated from the break-ins. The area rug's floral design made it difficult to separate. Colors and outlines blending in with the gems. Carpeted roses now had pierced pedals. Thorns wearing charm bracelets. The rug's border bedazzled with stud earrings.

Lena skimmed her palm across the floor rug, collecting gems in the process. She tossed the finds in her other hand. Fanning out her fingers, her hand was a windshield wiper, gliding left to right, cupping the score in the process.

Barb tossed a lariat-style necklace. The knot loosening to extend the length, it elongated the closer it got to Brittney. A charm bracelet flew toward Lena,

Drama Dolls

causing her to flinch. "Matches your shirt," Barb said, laughing. The calmest part of the heists was discovering what they had stolen. Each of them was in a relaxed state. The excitement overwhelming. It was having a secret only to themselves.

Brittney's inner voice, it was ecstatic. This was its favorite part. The nostalgia, it allowed Brittney inside to temporarily be distracted.

Pointing down to a stack near her, Barb said, "Bracelets over here in this pile." She recoiled when Lena returned the favor.

Rotating her arm like a catapult, Lena took aim and then fired. Shiny circles soared through the air. Bangles zipping by, each with a higher velocity. A variety of chain bracelets, they caused Barb to duck.

Bead, mesh, rolo, wheat, and byzantine chains directed toward Barb. Scale-like snake chain bracelets pinched her skin from the narrowly held links.

A gem fight was ensuing.

Brittney retrieved the jewelry pieces as Lena threw them, returning them back into the piles.

"Ow!" Barb said, turning her face away from the assault. A lobster clasp from a bracelet hurling through the air, it scuffed Barb's mask. Arms in the air, surrendering, she said, "I give up!"

Lena celebrated by seat dancing on the floor. Arms in ninety degree angles, fists closed, her shoulders bobbed up and down. She swayed left to right to a rhythm only she could hear. Lena's dancing made Brittney smile.

"Beautiful!" Brittney said.

Returning to posture, Barb said, "Dangerous! But totally beautiful."

After the dance, Lena flung her mask. A slow-motion, wrinkled face with a muted expression zipped toward Brittney. It hit her square in the nose. A hint of Chance Eau Tendre burning Brittney's nostrils.

Lena fell back in laughter. Adjusting her disguise, Brittney began to laugh as well.

Mimicking its owner, the voice of sympathetic reason laughed.

Lena's heart-shaped face – high cheekbones with full lips, and strong jaw – it was a permanent mask itself. Her skin was porcelain. She was a picturesque beauty. Almond shaped eyes looking up to the ceiling, Lena's body calmed. The laughter subsided.

Brittney had met Lena at a bereavement group for those who had lost loved ones suddenly. Married to a white-collar executive, Lena spent the majority of her day shopping online. Credit card number here, shipping address same as billing, click for overnight delivery.

Drama Dolls

Comparing products and reading reader reviews were a full-time job.

For Lena, cardboard boxes appeared on the front steps. Everything from clothes, workout shoes, Yoga mats, and watches, they only required a signature for acceptance. Lena's favorite purchase was jewelry. The reason she enjoyed the burglaries so much. She had an equal opportunity relationship with carcanets, chokers, and torcs, or neck rings. Lena acquired armlets, bangles, and chatelaines. Anything that caught her eyes, she bought.

A trophy wife, her role was to be arm candy for her husband at company events. And to be arm candy, you had to look the part.

An unlimited budget to keep her happy while her husband traveled and worked late. Vacuuming on her own schedule, if at all. When she did, Lena used a low noise, 1200 watt vacuum valued at eight hundred dollars.

Cleaning the kitchen while the daytime talk shows dished out advice, Lena lived her life the way she wanted. Chores that ran into next week, there was not ever accountability. Looking pretty had its advantages. Being sexually available had its perks.

While steaming vegetables, a phone call from a corporate lawyer relayed the accident in short sentences. Words easy to comprehend. Non-lawyer speak.

"And just like that," she said, speaking to the circle of the bereavement group's unnamed chairs, "I found myself alone."

The support group, a meeting place for victims to connect, each of the members consoled her. "Sorry for your loss." Then, "Welcome to the group." The members all had something in common. They all had lost someone.

"All the expensive things I had couldn't cure my loneliness," Lena said.

Regular people joined by a common link. Death, it affected all people, all occupations. Accountants, cooks, realtors, secretaries. A support group for all to grieve. Doctors, the unemployed, teenagers. Dying could happen to anyone.

Some of the grievers were strangers, only seeing each other anonymously. Others, they gathered regularly for coffee, online chats, or in Brittney/Jeffrey and Lena's case, burglaries.

Breathing deeply, Lena continued. "The first few months were emotional. I broke down for no reason. Different times of the day." Watching commercials with couples, Lena wept. "I couldn't control myself," she said. Everything was a trigger for Lena.

To expedite the healing process, Lena decided to remove herself from her husband's memory. She donated

Drama Dolls

sentimental items to secondhand stores. Items from her wedding; wine glasses given as gifts, unused kitchen appliances, her dress to a costume store. Replacing living room sets with brand new pieces, she maxed out her credit cards with miscellaneous purchases. Her sleep schedule got disrupted; sleeping for only a movie's length at night only to pace the house in the darkness. Cat naps throughout the day left no time for life. Acting out in unusual ways, Lena felt lost. Finding a friend in Jeffrey, she recharged her batteries. A sense of belonging brushing over her.

"That was how you dealt with your husband's loss," the group leader said. "That's perfectly natural. We all deal with grief differently." The group leader said, "The only thing that will cure you is time. So, please," he said, "occupy your time with distractions."

Once reality hit, Lena comprehended that she wasn't special after all. That her life had little value, if any at all. "Nobody would hire me," she said. "Didn't realize that not having skills would be the end of me." Sulking into her chair, she said, "Prettiness doesn't pay the bills."

A real estate agent, her twin brother died in a car accident. Falling asleep behind the wheel, his car drifting across the yellow line, he never woke up. "This may sound weird," the realtor said, "but I felt him die." Waking up in the middle of the night, body sweating, stiff and fully alert, she said her body felt as if collapsed inside. "Like something was pushing my head into my kidneys." She was compressing like an accordion. Crying, her story becoming more dynamic with each word, she said, "My head, caving into my body with brute force."

A pharmacist whose son was murdered closed her eyes and inhaled. "When your life hits rock bottom," she said, clutching the crucifix around her neck, "you have to find the strength to move on." She looked up to the ceiling, through the roof and into the heavens. "God has shown me the way." Locking her gaze onto the realtor, she said, "And He will show you the way too."

Lena reminded Jeffrey of his wife. Physically the characteristics were scary. Nearly the same build, Lena was more athletic. Thighs toned from working out regularly. Hair down to her back, blonde with a trace of sandy brown. Dimples up and down her cheeks. She had pear shaped breasts as far as Jeffrey/Brittney could tell. A similar sense of humor and when they laughed, their noses would crinkle the same way. When she laughed, her eyes disappeared under her eyelids.

While Lena rolled around on the living room floor, Barb sorted the jewelry into orderly piles. Barb's mask, creased in between her crossed legs, as she picked

Drama Dolls

and placed accordingly.

"What a night!" Lena said, lying in corpse pose. Her arms and legs flat on the floor.

There were five stages of grief: denial, anger, bargaining, depression, and acceptance. When She passed, for Jeffrey, for Brittney, the five stages were a laundry cycle of emotions. All coming together, at different intervals, mixing together at various periods. After Brittney had heard of the death, the hours succeeding were forever and an hour of disdain toward anything or anyone who was not grieving.

Memories flashing through in no particular order, Brittney attempted to hold on to Her as long as possible. Recollections sparked by a couple holding hands, they appeared without warning.

Sitting alone organizing necklaces and bracelets, Brittney's body deflated. The inner Brittney, feeling sorry for itself, started singing Eric Carmen's "All By Myself." Building up to a cry, Brittney crouched in her spot, never allowing herself to ruin the other Dolls' fun.

The night, it got away from them. Fatigue was approaching. Brittney wanted them to leave. She wanted to check on Emily. She excused herself from the scene to find her, to find Emily.

Barb eyed Brittney out. Her smile disappearing without hesitation. Her behavior, it shifted from elation to anger. Fuming inside as her nostrils breathed heavily in and out. Waiting until Brittney disappeared completely from the room, Barb pointed her finger toward Lena. In an accusing manner, she said, "What the fuck?"

Rolling up into a sitting position, Lena said, "What?"

Cutting a look to where she last saw Brittney, Barb slowly turned her head toward Lena, and said, "This crazy nut job bringing that freak show?"

Her head sinking, the side of her mouth curling upward, Lena said, "Are you joking?"

Picking up her mask in one swift motion, Barb slammed the plastic accessory down to the floor. Her eyebrows lowering, her front teeth showing, Barb's eyes began to squint. She said, "Does it look like I'm fucking joking?"

Offended, her mouth dropping open, Lena said, "Emily." Enunciating each word clearly, she said, "Her name is Emily."

"Whatever!" Barb said, her teeth clenching.

A brief staredown led to an awkward silence. The sound of a door slamming in the garage disrupted the tension and forced both burglar Dolls to regain focus.

Drama Dolls

"And then he introduced us to each other?" Rubbing the top row of teeth with her tongue, Barb's lips puckered. Her hands in front of her, fingers spread out, Barb said, "This is getting out of hand!"

A door latching in the distance, Barb and Lena could tell Brittney was close to returning. Lena leaned in close to Barb and said, "It's not for you to decide."

The room was filled to the ceiling with stolen goods. Piles as high as their upper torsos. An inventory of bad deeds.

"You need to fucking stop," Lena said. Her voice, going from soft to a whisper/scream, she said, "This is not about you. This is about Jeffrey." Straightening a stack of bracelets that had fallen over, Lena said, "His fucking wife just died!"

Sitting between empty pillowcases, surrounded by a bathtub worth of jewels, the two had a brief staredown. Without either person budging and before Brittney could return, Barb curled the side of her lip upward. A cold expression, a feeling of defeat, she said, "Fine!"

Calming the situation, Lena's voice softening, she said, "Just give him some time." A glazed look on Barb's face appeared. Lena said, "Think about when you first met him. You two were a lot alike."

William was just as screwed up as Jeffrey. The problems were different but the results were the same. The lack of self-confidence from being overweight and physically unattractive was so strong that William found prettiness in a bag. An adult cheerleader costume purchased at a Halloween store started the fetish. Paintable white masks encouraged William to experiment with applying various combinations of makeup, color schemes that worked. Once he became a pro at this, William turned to hair.

The crop of hair falling out on his own head, William noticed a horseshoe pattern forming on his scalp. Using cloth tape to measure the hairline from the base of his neck up to the hairline on his forehead, William envisioned a full head of hair again. The cloth tape extending from his forehead over the crown of his scalp and down toward his nape, William concluded by measuring from ear to ear.

Transferring the dimensions to a wig block, pushing in cotton ribbons to the wooden head stump, William's new hair was within reach. Applying wet cotton lace and stitching it into the ribbons, the final step was for William to select hair. Deciding against using real hair,

Drama Dolls

William recalled the little girl at the park combing her Barbie Doll's mane. How pretty and shiny it was. How brushing it drew the biggest smile on the young child's face.

The insecure man settled on Saran and Kanekalon, the same material found on plastic Dolls, hoping to transfer that exact same happiness to himself. The notion of having a multitude of colors fascinated William. From light platinum blonde to an amber coppery blonde and from a chocolate brown to a basic black, there was not ever a day where William was at a loss for colors.

Playing dress-up boosted his self-esteem. His confidence high, William began taking care of himself, working out, and staying positive.

When he met Jeffrey, Jeffrey allowed him to be beautiful.

Empathizing with Jeffrey/Brittney relaxed her. Barb's demeanor changed. She was now curious, engaging Lena to discuss her own loss. Emotions subsiding, Barb's heart slowed its pace. Staring into Lena's eyes, she said, "How long did it take for you to get over your husband?"

Recognizing the change in Barb's attitude, Lena

smiled. She said, "Longer than this."

Barb nodded her head in agreement. Her eyes drifted toward the floor. She was beginning to understand where Lena was coming from.

"Let's just give him some time," Lena said. Picking up random necklaces and holding them up in front of her, she said, "No matter how ridiculous things get."

Pursing her lips, Barb said, "OK."

Cupping an item in her palm, Lena said, "Just remember, he's not thinking clearly."

To soften the mood, Lena flung a byzantine chain necklace in the direction of Barb. The thick accessory spun toward the unsuspecting cheerleader.

Ducking, her shoulders propping up and her head dropping south, Barb said, "Hey!"

Throwing expensive jewelry around was something Lena had grown accustomed to. The 14k gold, 6.50mm byzantine chain necklace valued at five grand was no exception. She had worn items twice the value for her husband.

Guarding her body from flying objects, Barb said, "I surrender. I surrender."

Brittney pulled Emily into the living room. Her arms locked under the comatose Drama Doll's shoulders.

Drama Dolls

Emily's legs dragged through a stack of bracelets. Rows of circles, piled high like poker chips, falling over from the contact.

Barb rolled her eyes.

Lena shot the discouraging cheerleader a glare. Her eyes piercing, the death stare non-verbally reminded Barb of their conversation.

"Sorry," Brittney said. Parting the stacks into sections with Emily's frame, Brittney heaved the unconscious doll onto the couch.

Lena stared at the scene; her peppy attitude slowly deflating.

The thrust from the throw had forced Brittney's mask to slide off center. Shaking her head, whipping it sharply, the plastic expression fell to the ground.

Lena's eyes moved from left to right. A look toward Barb, then to the resting Drama Doll, Lena said, "Well, we should probably get going."

Crouched with knees bent, Brittney adjusted Emily's dead weight on the couch. Never acknowledging the fact that she had company, live conscious company, Brittney did not hear Barb and Lena leave.

The room now quiet, Brittney and her obsession were alone. The fully uniformed doll was sleeping on the couch. Her mask facing up, Emily looked like a mannequin waiting to be placed in the store. She was a ghostly cheerleader.

Inside, the little voice, whispering into Brittney's eardrum, it said, "What about your wife?"

When Emily wasn't passed out, she was a work of art. Blackish straight hair pulled down tight on the sides of her face. Olive colored eyes the shape of water droplets. A triangular nose above her diamond molded lips, Emily, like Lena, did not need a mask to be beautiful.

Her skin was silky smooth, the color of white caramel.

Dimensionally, Emily's body was textbook. Her bust measured thirty-two inches. Torso curving down into a twenty-four-inch waist, and rounding out into thirty-three-inch hips. A size two dress with size seven shoes made her a goddess to be worshipped.

Brittney fought every urge to respect Her, never saying inappropriate remarks or attempting to come on to Emily. After tying Emily's right shoe, Brittney sat in the broken stacks of the heist and closed her eyes.

Unaccompanied, in the darkness of the room, the only light emanated from underneath the lampshade on the end table. Brittney's body shuddered. The tears had enveloped her face since dusk. Drops fell freely; they were a leaky faucet waiting to be turned off. Body shaking,

Drama Dolls

crying in the middle of the floor, Brittney reached for her mask so that Emily would not see her that way.

Stone still, a hollow expression on the outside. Inside, Brittney was a lost soul hoping to be saved.

The evening drawing to a close, Brittney picked up Emily and headed for the long flight upstairs.

Hanging from Brittney's back, the dead-weight arms were wrapped around Brittney's neck. Her legs were around Brittney's waist. Feet were kicking each stair that she passed.

Carrying dead weight was good for Brittney's thighs. Soon, she would have legs like both Barb and Lena.

The voice of reason, though, it was out of breath.

Halfway up, the heaviness causing her legs to burn, Brittney stopped for air. Her heart was racing. Chest pounding, the trek to the bedroom continued. Emily's foot caught the lip of a stair, pulling the struggling Brittney back, almost tumbling downward.

Rising up on her toes, the force from the thrust caused Emily's foot to fly forward into Brittney's calf. Falling off balance, Brittney grabbed the staircase railing and pulled herself straight. Rocking back and forth, the weight of the passed out cheerleader on her back, Brittney reclaimed her posture.

61

Exhaling quick, short breaths, Emily in tow, the journey continued forward.

The phone machine blinked. There were unheard messages waiting to be listened to. Phone calls needing to be returned. Brittney/Jeffrey's parents had called during each cup of coffee since his wife's death. When they didn't reach their son, the phone calls extended to brunch, then dinner, and then finally to all hours.

Single-line sentences such as, "Are you OK?" and "We're worried about you," and "Let us know if you need us." These messages vibrated off the empty house's walls.

Brittney's life hadn't always been that of a cheerleader. Jeffrey's life hadn't always been that of Brittney.

"Your father wanted a girl," his mother said over lunch. This was the first get together since Her death. Jeffrey's mother sipped her water, patting down her lips with a napkin. Mother's round wire-rim glasses sliding down the tip of her nose as she raised the glass to her face. Her skin wrinkled from the sun, makeup covering the sunspots that filled her cheeks. She said, "We tried after you but it just wasn't in God's plan."

Drama Dolls

The only child of two teachers, Jeffrey's importance was shuffled in with various students throughout his parents' tenures. After-school was spent contending for quality time while his mother graded papers. Competing with Jennifer, Sarah, Everett, Kyle the Teacher's Pet, the Redheaded Boy with Freckles, and Braces became a challenge. He competed with Logan, Ashley, the Hearing Impaired Boy, Half-Asian, and No-Neck Nathan. Jeffrey, he started acting out to get the educators' attention. Detention after school for skipping class. Minor thefts led to vandalism led to underage drinking. All to gain his parents' love.

His parents were forced to address the concern. Meetings with school officials turned to the recommendation of therapy visits. Although the attention was negative, Jeffrey outshined his competitors. Not that it was difficult. Jennifer never stayed after school, Kyle the Teacher's Pet could only suck up during the day, and Braces had his own issues with flossing.

Pushing her empty plate to the side of the table, Mother said, "It's probably why your relationship with him wasn't that great."

Sighing, Jeffrey said, "He was too involved in his own students' lives rather than mine." Sipping his lukewarm tea, he said, "The both of you were."

Shrugging her shoulders, as if the topic had no meaning at all, desensitized from years of "raising" children, Mother, she said, "So, how are you doing?"

The whole time Jeffrey had been married, the relationship with his parents was nonexistent. That first meeting was the most quality talk they'd had in time without end. Jeffrey's wife had encouraged him to call his folks regularly, saying that they should invite them over for dinner. Or tea. But there was never time.

Swallowing the rest of the peppermint tea, he said, "I'm moving forward every day." Placing his teacup on the edge of the table, he reached for a napkin and patted his lips. A stained lip impression wetting the napkin's surface made him smile. The lips reminded him of models who would apply a fresh coat of lipstick and then kiss a letter to their fans.

Jeffrey said, "I have no other choice but to move on."

His mother, finishing her glass of water, said, "It was a shame what happened to her."

The truth was that Her death had brought Jeffrey closer to his mother again. And even though they still did not have the relationship that She had wanted for her husband, Jeffrey and Mother were not miles away any longer.

Drama Dolls

The voice of silver lining reason, it said, "Let's keep on keeping on."

Now the question became, did dressing up like a cheerleader doll constitute "having a daughter"?

Continuing through the corridor of the house, the phone rang. Enduring the march ahead, the message through the machine said, "Hi, honey. Thought maybe you'd like to talk." Then a beep. The emptiness of the house was iridescently scary. Feeling alone in the oversized dwelling, the setting was both eerie and serene at the same time.

Turning the corner into the bedroom, dragging Emily through the doorway, Brittney kicked the door closed.

Tucked into bed, snug and under the covers, Brittney/Jeffrey's second wind hit. Emily's uniform and mask were in a pile on the floor as she slept curled up into a ball. With the mess of scattered clothing, Jeffrey's body energized, he started to clean. Nobody should see the room in that state.

Kicking underwear under the bed, tossing shirts into dressers, the area slowly came together. Pulling out a broom and dustpan, sweeping around the corners of the room, the pan collected dirt and random flies' corpses. Cleaning the room put Jeffrey at ease. Bringing it back to how She liked it was always the goal when he cleaned.

Moving around the house, the broom pushed up against the walls, the dust piling into little hills, the widower swept the entire perimeter. Combining the dirt together and brushing them into the dust pan, the filth led him down the staircase.

Each stair, and in between each spindle, was brushed until the debris disappeared into the pan. Working the brush around the main floor's border, mountains of muck contained dirty piles of hair, random bobby pins, and earring backs from previous heists. Sweeping alone, the house's appearance improved drastically.

A necklace swept out from underneath the love seat sparkled in the dirt. Stopping to pick it up, holding it up to the lamp's glow, the charm glass locket blinded Jeffrey.

Blowing off the strands of hair and dust, he placed the necklet on the end table.

Stepping back, Jeffrey howled. "Ahh!" Lifting his foot behind him, an indent in his skin, Jeffrey scanned the floor to see the lost earring back from earlier. He cupped the back in his palm and then continued the task of

Drama Dolls

cleaning the entire house before Emily woke up.

Once he finished with the sweeping, the floor's coating appeared bland from the broom's bristles. Grabbing a bucket and filling it with warm water and white vinegar, Jeffrey dropped in a mop to dampen it. Wringing it dry, the water drops playing a melody into the puddle, he stopped short.

Above him, the phone rang until the machine picked up. Jeffrey waited for a voice. "Hey there," Lena's disembodied voice said. "I just wanted to see if everything was OK." There was a slight pause. Jeffrey, walking closer to the voice, heard the message continue. "Anyway, hope all is well. Call me if you want."

A block away from Jeffrey's house, sitting in her car in a gas station parking lot, Lena stared at the outgoing phone call to her friend. The call register blinked at thirty seconds, the duration of the call going to voicemail. Worried that William was right, she justified her action by relating her own experience with losing a spouse.

After the truth hit Lena, her venture into the real world was challenging. Unable to find a job that paid enough to support her lifestyle, she phoned a financial advisor to talk about her options. Losing her husband was tough, but living through the aftermath was a harsher reality.

Waiting on tables for less than a meal's tip, she could not afford the life she had built with her husband. Parts of her felt worthless for even letting her life get to that point. But, as the group leader of bereavement once told her, "Something drastic always has to happen for you to change your habits." Lena just did not believe that her husband's death was the drastic event looming around the corner.

Dropping her head down to her chest, dressed head to toe in cheerleading attire, she began to feel sorry for herself. Meeting Jeffrey had allowed her to move on. Jeffrey meeting William had allowed him to move on. They all needed each other to save themselves from being alone, being discarded again from the "normalcy" of society.

A cop tapping the car window with his knuckle startled Lena back to reality.

The green glow of the shelter above the gas pumps blinding her, she rolled down the window to address the officer.

The flashlight shining in her face, she squinted

Drama Dolls

from the circle of light.

"Ma'am," the police official said. "The gas station's clerk called and wanted someone to check up on you." Spinning the flashlight's glow into the car's interior, the officer leaned in closer to Lena.

His eyebrows lowering, his bottom lip dropping open, he said, "Are you wearing a cheerleader uniform?"

In the backseat were pom-poms. The accessories' feathers fanned out like a peacock to show their full form. Stuffed into the space behind Lena's seat, on the floor mat, were empty bags crumple stacked on top of each other.

Her eyes bulging, shifting rapidly left to right, Lena, quick thinking, said, "Yes. I coach cheerleading for a local high school squad that is competing in a national championship."

The cop pulled his head back. The flashlight swirled around the automobile. Using the overhead alien glow as guidance, the police officer moved his head left to right to see into the car.

Channeling her inner cheerleader, Lena said, "Back to back champs."

Eyebrows furrowing, the cop, waving cheerleader out of the car, said, "Ma'am, please step out of the automobile."

Stepping out of the car, Lena struck a pose.

Alarmed, the officer reached for his gun in its holster, ready for action.

Arranged to begin a routine, she put her finger up, signaling the public servant to wait. "Hang on," she said. "Don't shoot."

Reaching for her pom-poms, her body half in the car, Lena grabbed the accessories and then slid back out. Standing erect, holding a pom-pom in each hand, she returned to form. Her legs spread, feet even with her waist, she raised one arm out. Stretching her closed fist out high, her other arm rested on her hip. Lena said, "This is known as the 'go' pose."

Backing up slowly, one step at a time, the police officer stayed prepared, pointing the flashlight toward Lena while his free hand stayed close to his gun.

Inside the gas station, the clerk working the register watched the entire ordeal. He laughed behind the glass, jerking his head down and shaking his head at the sight.

The cop slowly craned his neck toward the lighted store window and then back toward the posing cheerer.

"Ready?" Lena said, body straightening, her arms falling to the side. "OK."

Shaking the pom-poms in front of her, her arms straight and parallel to the pavement, Lena cheered.

Drama Dolls

"Who's the best squad in the whole wide world?" The peppy cheerer twisted her hips to the right. Her left leg kicked up. Her raised knee bending. Lena's arms shot up into a high "V" and then fell back down to the front of her body. Holding the pom-poms stiff, the plastic feathers shook from the movement.

Pulling down her leg, returning to her body's original "ready" pose, Lena screamed, "Bayside High! Bayside High!" She clapped in rhythm as she continued screaming, "Bayside High, Bayside High!"

With the police officer stunned back into his heels, Lena proceeded into a stretch of cheerleader poses she'd practiced with Jeffrey.

Pumped up, her adrenaline rushing, Lena did the low clasp, opposite the high "V" but with her hands clasped together pointing down toward the ground. Instead of the high "V" above her head, the position was mirrored, lowered below the waist.

Twisting her hips, Lena groaned from the sudden movement. Bending slightly, knees were soft. Lena's one arm still in low clasp position, the opposite arm shot up high into the air. Lena, she said, "This is referred to the 'K' pose."

In the store's window behind her, the clerk pointed out toward Lena. His other hand was covering his mouth. He jumped up and down in excitement, his body recoiling inward at the same time.

Returning to low clasp position, instead of the low "V" to the concrete, she crossed her arms together. Breathing heavily, Lena said to the cop, "Do you know what this pose is called?"

Shrugging his shoulders, his mouth curling down into a frown, the police officer said, "It looks like you're making an 'X.'"

Lena jumped up into a scissor kick, her arms punching into the air. At the top of her leap, she said, "Ya-a-a-ay copper!" Landing, she returned to the low "X" position. The quick motion caused her to wince in pain. Even though she had practiced the cheerleader moves, doing them in rapid succession was a different animal.

The overaged cheerleader finished her demonstration with daggers, her two arms in ninety degree angles in front of her chest; and then touchdown, her arms straight up in the air like a football referee signaling a score.

She then went into a low inverted "V," and then ended with the bucket pose, her legs spread out and straight, her one arm bent at the elbow as high as her chest and parallel to her shoulders, and her remaining arm extended out sideways, in line with her bent arm.

Drama Dolls

Statue-still, catching her breath, Lena stood tall, stiff as could be.

The cop, eying the laughing clerk and then turning his head back toward Lena, tucked the flashlight under his armpit and slow clapped.

A faint scream coming from the inside of the gas station filtered out into the parking lot. The clerk pushed a button, turning on the speaker above the gas pumps. He said, "That was awesome!" After the police officer's slow clapping died to a halt, the clerk said, "But, please, there is no loitering."

Before her legs could cramp, Lena softened her knees and slowly bowed to the officer.

Trading in the Toyota Corolla for a Chevy Corvette was a long time coming. Even though the winters consisted of sub-zero weather and knee-high snow drifts, the sports car removed wrinkles from Jeffrey's age. Gone were the perceptions of predictability, middle-age, and being safe.

Trading miles per gallon for speed wasn't practical. It was a true sign of aging. Dying your hair when it turned white, shaving the gray out of your beard, there were always ways to look youthful.

The decision to unload the Corolla was challenging for Jeffrey. The gas-saving vehicle had always been reliable throughout the ever changing weather patterns that hit his area.

It had, after all, two rows of seats, the ability to seat five comfortably - six if there were children involved – and safety ratings and cost savings over the lifespan of the car. These were factors that Jeffrey couldn't ignore. The reasons he opted for a Corolla to begin with.

The Corvette, though, had power and intense fast speed. With great cornering ability, the 'Vette tested high on road tests. The luxury features and entertainment system were icing on Jeffrey's proverbial cake.

The voice of cool reasoning said, "No. Brainer."

Overall, the decision had nothing to do with features; rather, it had everything to do with Jeffrey working through the pain caused by his wife's death. At least, this was how he justified the purchase.

Looking out the window, the silver sports car was partially covered by shingles. Parked in front of the house for a random passerby to admire, the status gave Jeffrey

Drama Dolls

strength. He felt on top of the world with the speedster, oftentimes driving the scenic route to and from work just to get more eyeballs on him.

For the inner voice, the status gave it a disembodied boner.

Jeffrey leaned in to see the glowing top of the automobile, a spotlight circle caused by the street light nearby. Sleep deprivation mocking him, his balance teetering back and forth, Jeffrey closed his eyes and dozed off in a standing position. His heart rate increased, and before he could fall into a deep coma sleep, Jeffrey jolted his eyes open. The burning of his eyes caused him to blink. Strained to the point they became itchy.

He slid into bed next to Emily, who had transitioned from her "passed out" stage to a "sleeping peacefully" phase. Since Her death, sleep was a limited resource waiting to be discovered. Hoping to capitalize on the short period of sleeping while standing, Jeffrey closed his eyes and attempted to clear his mind.

The problem was Jeffrey's brain kept him awake. Every "what if?" scenario racing through his thoughts, he puzzled together situations that sometimes existed and sometimes were random figments of his imagination. Piecing together a logical explanation of why his wife could have died, Jeffrey often came up empty as the facts and fictions never became actual facts but instead stayed a conjoining mix of practical and make-believe ideas.

Tossing, turning, kicking the blanket off his legs, nights were spent staring at the ceiling. Hating Emily because she could sleep. Counting down each minute until sunrise.

Unable to go under, Jeffrey walked to the "his" of the "his & her" closets. With every inch of wood already swept, Jeffrey assessed the next situation. Drooping on one side of the walk-in was a row of button-down shirts organized by color. Hangers facing the same way, the front of the shirts closed, garments were held together by the top button. Whites, yellows, blues, and then greens, each dress shirt ironed straight; ready to be worn.

Opposite the shirts were slacks pinched by pant hanger clips. Dangling down the length of the inseams, the colors coordinated with their counterparts across the walk-in.

Over top of the rods, shelves spanned the closet. Shoes were in pairs, from dress to casual. Facing away from Jeffrey when he walked in, the heels were at his eye level. Also used as mini-storage, boxes stacked against the back wall. Jeffrey tapped the stack of boxes with his foot, forgetting momentarily what was inside them. When they slid away from him, he observed that they were empty.

Drama Dolls

Evaluating the apparel, sliding each shirt individually to the end of the rod, Jeffrey pulled down the articles considered outdated. Yanking shirts off the hangers, pulling pants from the clips, he tossed them behind. The rods now three quarters bare, the discarded attire was shaped like a volcano on the wood surface.

Feeling accomplished, Jeffrey stood above the pile of the throwaways. Beating his chest, one closed fist at a time as if he was a gorilla, he circled his lips around an invisible cigar and grunted out loud.

The noise apparently did not bother Emily, as her body remained in the same position that Jeffrey had dumped her in. The thumps on his chest getting louder, his grunts echoing off the walls, Jeffrey started to hop on one foot, alternating his legs until he developed a rhythm. Every other jump, his foot slid on rejected shirts from the closet. The stinging in his ankle reemerging, the childish cheerleader stopped the unnecessary bouncing.

Collecting the heap of fabric and depositing the clothing into the garbage can, excitement faded from the heist and impersonating a hairy beast. Tiredness became prevalent.

Jeffrey sighed deeply, sleep finally in his future. Climbing into bed, the morning coming soon, a car door slammed, startling him back alive.

Jason Tanamor

His lower body underneath the covers, almost positioned in a resting position, Jeffrey mouthed the word, "Nooooo." Dropping his head to his chest, closing his eyes sharply, he said, "I just want to sleep."

Giving in to his curiosity, Jeffrey walked over to the window. Peeling back the curtain, his face half covered, Jeffrey stared through the tree, onto the lighted pavement.

Jeffrey saw the neighbor kid light a cigarette. The boy was standing around a rusted Pontiac Grand-Am. Laughing with a shorter boy, silhouetted by the lone street light, the neighbor's shadow inhaled a drag and then released.

Their voices were low. Every third word was audible.

Watching from afar, Jeffrey saw the shorter boy fire up a bowl. Manmade from a crushed aluminum pop can, holes poked in the crushed portion of the can, a stash of pot burning over the holes, the pipe was made in a relatively short period of time.

The shorter boy sucked out the drug from the drinking spout. Deep into his lungs, the marijuana fried his insides. The drug sizzling on the can, he passed the Mountain Dew pipe to the neighbor kid.

The aroma of marijuana floated through Jeffrey's

Drama Dolls

bedroom windows. His eyes tightening, the pot gave Jeffrey a contact high. Closing his eyes, the teenagers' voices were getting louder, clearer.

"Sweet ride!" the shorter boy said. The neighbor and friend walked over to the Corvette and stood around it, admiring the car's splendor. "Check out the rims, Alex." The shorter boy was kneeling before the rear wheel when Alex made the turn. Pot getting stronger, the shorter boy inhaled and then passed the bowl to Alex.

Flicking his cigarette out into the street, the neighbor pursed his lips and sucked in the drug. Alex, with a sarcastic tone, he said, "Just bought this. His wife died so apparently you trade in your car for a 'Vette." He slowly exhaled the smoke and then shrugged. "He's fucking weird."

Peeking into the car's window, the shorter boy scanned the entire inside in one turn.

Walking up to the boys, their backs toward him as the teenaged pair appreciated the automobile, Jeffrey said, "What're you two doing?"

The neighbor turned to address Jeffrey. "Hey, dude. Just checkin' out your ride."

"Nice car, man!" the shorter boy said, reaching for a hit.

The pot making him dizzy, Jeffrey thanked them.

His eyes turning red, constricting inside his eye sockets, Jeffrey's eyes rolled back into his head.

"You're up kinda late," Alex said.

Eyes coming back into view, vision going in and out, the lack of sleep fucking with him, Jeffrey closed his eyes for a second. Holding up his finger, Jeffrey zoned out.

Alex cocked his head to his buddy.

The first time Jeffrey smoked pot was at Paul's house. The group had acquired a bag from a janitor who worked at the high school. The janitor, attempting to make money from his side business, cracked a joke with Paul, asking what the point of being in high school was if you weren't actually getting high.

"Get it?" he said. "High school."

The two hit it off, and within a week, Paul was a regular buyer. Introducing the marijuana was easy. Wait until his buddies were drunk off Milwaukee's Best and then slip them a joint while jamming out to the Doors and Steve Miller. Adding in, "What's the point of being in high school if you aren't actually getting high?" in the process.

Paul, his nickname became Space Cowboy. And Jeffrey, he became a space cadet after his first hit. Addicted

Drama Dolls

to the high, the space cadet indulging the most out of his pals, Jeffrey found himself either drunk or stoned the majority of his time in high school.

Alex, clearing his throat, projecting his voice outward, repeated, "I said, 'You're up kinda late.'"

His finger still in mid-air, Jeffrey blinked his eyes until his head cleared. Noticing the looks on the boys' faces, their eyes shifting complemented by empty expressions, Jeffrey pulled down his hand.

Craning his head toward the bedroom, Jeffrey said, "The old lady is passed out." Shrugging, a smirk on his face, he said, "Chicks!"

The boys, they lowered their eyebrows in unison, turning toward each other. Concerned looks on their mugs, they returned to lock gazes with Jeffrey. The marijuana smoke disappearing into the air, the shorter boy took another hit.

Alex said, "Didn't your wife just die?"

Eyes enlarging, Jeffrey tapped his foot in a nervous fashion. "I, uh, mean, a friend is passed out," he said. Jeffrey's head was a sprinkler on a dry lawn. Swiveling back and forth from the neighbor to his buddy, his eyes a branched out veiny red, Jeffrey said, "She's just checking up on me."

The shorter boy blew out the smoke toward Jeffrey's face. Jeffrey closed his eyes and inhaled the drug. He could feel his eyes compressing, cracking inside their sockets. In his brain, "The Joker" played, *Some people call me the space cowboy, yeah, Some call me the gangster of love; Some people call me Maurice, Cause I speak of the pompitous of love.*

Nodding his head, up and down in a slow motion, Alex the neighbor said, "Well, I guess we'll be—"

Cutting him off, shaking his head, Jeffrey said, "Wanna go for a ride?"

The two young men looked at each other, then to Jeffrey.

Pointing to the homemade bowl, motioning with his fingers in a smoking gesture, lips circled, Jeffrey said, "May I?" The boys did nothing. In fact, they did not know how to react. "C'mon," Jeffrey said. "I can be cool."

Hesitating, Alex was cautious. The only other contact the two had had was during Jeffrey's marriage.

Loud music late into the night from the garage, the elder knew the neighbor boy's parents were out for the

Drama Dolls

evening. Classic rock echoing out of the boom box speakers, the music mixed with a chattering of voices. Kansas sang "Carry On Wayward Son," as Alex and his friends joined in on the lyrics.

Laughter from the boys rang into the air. The noise traveled through the atmosphere and into Jeffrey's house. Off key, collectively, they sang.

There was a loud bang. Alex's friend fell to the ground after jumping up and down into a garbage can. The singing transformed into hilarity.

Their voices raised, the sound was getting louder and louder.

Inside the kitchen, Jeffrey looked out the window to the ruckus's direction. Standing still, his arms on his hips, the silently fuming husband did not hear his wife slink up behind him. "They're having fun, Jeffrey," she said. "Just let them be."

Hid body tensing, nostrils flared, Jeffrey said, "How do they even know this song? How old are they, like sixteen?"

His wife, shaking her head, said, "Silly husband. You were listening to the Doors and Queen at their age." Jeffrey didn't budge. His non-action prompted Her to rub her hand up and down his back. "I think those boys are a lot like you were. So, give them a break and just let them be."

Beer cans shot out of the garage. The tin material jangling on the street. A bottle of Miller Lite rolled down the slope of the driveway. Followed by another. Crushed Bud cans flung out like saucers. Some landed in a tree. Others in the yard. One spinning so fast it curved from the velocity and nearly hit a parked car's windshield.

A long haired boy with a smoke hanging from his lips ran out of the garage. Trash can in hand, he sat it upright in the middle of the driveway where the slope evened out.

A game was happening.

"Whoever can make the most cans," he said, his Camel falling out of his mouth. Reaching down to retrieve the cigarette, he stuck it behind his ear. "The most cans in the garbage wins."

A team of Bud cans whizzed out into the driveway. Coors saucers followed. The clinking was a snare drum at times. Round makeshift coasters on the cement. The sloping pavement looked like an indoor rock climbing wall with the crushed aluminum placed sporadically around the lot.

Following the screams of enjoyment, Jeffrey displayed his presence. Standing in the driveway, arms crossed, Jeffrey stared down the group.

Drama Dolls

The boys slowly halted their actions. One of the boys ran to the radio and turned it down. The music softly fading out into the next.

"Thank you," Jeffrey said. He looked out into the driveway and said, "I expect this mess will be cleaned up before your parents get home?"

Alex nodded. His friends nodded. One boy laughed.

Jeffrey stood a few more moments, a look of disappointment on his face. He said, "Very good."

With Metallica blasting from the radio, the song "One" with its double bass drum pounding through the boys' chests, the long-haired boy started to bang his head. Another joined in and played air guitar.

Jeffrey shook his head and walked back to his house.

There was never communication after the incident. The only exchange was the polite head nod entering and exiting the house.

The silence becoming awkward, Alex shrugged. "Cool." He offered up the pot and the three killed the pipe. For Jeffrey, the night was continuing to be a good one. Without wasting any time, the trio piled into the Corvette. Jeffrey revved the engine, the feeling of man testicles hitting them in the face.

"Fucking awesome!" the shorter boy said. The windows rolled down, Alex and the shorter boy were sharing a bucket seat. Their arms hanging out the car's window, the teenagers could not wait to see what the car could do.

Forcefully stepping down on the gas pedal, the car peeled out of the parking spot. Nearly hitting the curbs along the boulevard, the sports car fishtailed for a half block and then eventually straightened out. The late hour contributed to the streets being empty. Every stretch of straight roads, Jeffrey floored it, reaching high speeds he would have never attained in his Corolla.

The shorter boy turned on the Bose stereo. The volume, high enough to hear music but low enough to make out words, caused the young potheads to look at Jeffrey.

Feeling the stares on the side of his neck, Jeffrey turned up the volume. Inside the CD player was a Steve Miller collection. Guitar riffs pushing out of the Bose speakers, the sound filled the inside of the 'Vette. The joyriders rocked out to the music.

Jeffrey, one hand on the top of the steering wheel,

Drama Dolls

the other out the window tapping the side of the door, sang along with the track.

Alex pumped his fist to the beat and the shorter boy played air drums. The Corvette's speed accelerating, turning corners effortlessly, Jeffrey felt alive and was not obsessing about Her or Emily or even Lena or William.

Running through a four way stop sign earned their trust. Speeding down weaving sections of road kept them engaged. Taking a right turn at a highway speed forced Alex to extend his arm out the window. His fingers making devil horns, Alex screamed, "Woo!"

Steve Miller now singing "Take The Money and Run."

The shorter kid, he just smiled with his mouth open. The fast motion of the car, the frequent turns, and the fact that he was higher than a kite, they all contributed to him leaning over Alex, stretching his upper body out so that his head could reach out the window, and then hurling out into the atmosphere at ninety five miles per hour.

Hearing the jerking of the shorter boy's body go into a full blown seizure of vomiting, Jeffrey sped up, surpassing the one hundred miles per hour mark.

The shorter boy, in between BOO LAHs and inverted swallows, said, "Slow down!"

Leaning as close to the middle as possible, away

from the window, Alex said, "No! Speed up!"

And Jeffrey, attempting to not have vomit splattered on the side of his 'Vette, stepped down on the pedal so hard the ball of his foot began to cramp.

The warm air entering the car hit each joyrider in the face.

The shorter boy's vision became blurry. His head was floating. Eyelids falling down over his eyeballs. Alex, leaning into Jeffrey, watched his buddy judder into a frenzy. Watching the convulsing boy disco centipede in mid-air, Alex couldn't help but laugh.

The car slowed down to a highway speed. The car approached a business district.

The shorter boy's vomit now a dry heave, with his mouth sticky and his throat dry, he slowly started to feel better. Vision restoring slowly, the shorter boy could identify his surroundings.

A gas station was in sight. A faint smell of cheeseburgers lingered in the car. Alex's lips curled downward. He said, "Fucking gross, dude."

The shorter boy, swallowing until he built enough saliva, said, "Sorry. That was from this afternoon."

Pulling into a parking spot, Jeffrey said, "Who needs beer?"

Squished into one seat, the shorter boy, his thighs

Drama Dolls

on top of each other, said, "Beer!" Alex just laughed. The post-puker boy, turning to Alex said, "What? My stomach is empty now."

"Let me guess," Jeffrey said, "Bud? Miller Lite? Coors?"

Exiting the car, the shorter boy slid off Alex to stretch his legs. He said, "Whatever you buy, I'll drink it."

Jeffrey, anxious to hang out, said, "Sounds good." He disappeared into the store.

Alex, sitting shotgun, checked out the car's interior. Looking over at the dashboard, the steering wheel's center with the Corvette logo, he admired the car's gauges.

Leaning back toward the passenger seat, Alex grabbed the stick shift. Talking to himself, he said, "Nice."

Opening up the glove compartment, Alex found a tube of lipstick. Next to it, a tiny makeup pouch zipped closed. He twisted the base of the lipstick and watched it extend upward. Replacing the tube, he reached for the makeup pouch.

"What do you got there?" the shorter boy said.

Removing his hand, closing the glove compartment, Alex said, "Nothing."

"Wasn't sure what you wanted so I bought all three," Jeffrey said, emerging from the storefront. A six pack of bottles each, Jeffrey handed them to the shorter boy and walked around to the driver's side.

Slithering in the car, both hands filled with alcohol, the shorter boy twisted off a bottle cap and handed the beer to Alex. He reached for another one, removed the cap and then handed it to Jeffrey.

"Thank you kind sir," Jeffrey said. Taking a swig of the beer, Jeffrey licked his lips and said, "Ahh!"

Alex held up his Miller Lite. Both Jeffrey and the shorter boy clanked their bottles together. The three toasting to a good night.

Pulling out of the parking lot, the Corvette racing down side streets, the passengers downed their drinks.

"Where we going?" Alex said.

Turning down random streets, cutting through various neighborhoods of houses, Jeffrey said, "A place I used to go to with my wife."

Alex and the shorter boy looked at each other. The shorter boy, coming down from his high, feeling a bit nervous, said, "You're not going to want to have sex with us, are you?"

Jeffrey laughed out loud. His beer half gone, he said, "No, it's just a cool view of the sunrise."

"Why would we want—"

Alex nudged his friend.

Drama Dolls

The shorter boy, stopping in mid-sentence, looked at Alex.

And the neighbor kid, he did nothing but shake his head.

Steve Miller played underneath the quietness. The car cruising toward the lookout point, Jeffrey downed the rest of his bottle. He said, "I'd just think you'd like the view." Flinging the bottle out the window, Jeffrey floored it.

Alex, up for anything at this hour, also coming off his buzz, said, "No man. Sounds cool."

Looking over at Alex, Jeffrey flashed a smile. Turning up the volume, Jeffrey continued the drive. The 'Vette's speed well above the limit.

The sunrise made Jeffrey happy. Smiling into the giant orange glow rising up the sky, the three boys at heart sat back in their seats, drinking beer, and enjoyed the scenery.

Each down from his respective marijuana buzz, the trio sat in silence, watching the ball of fire expand into the horizon.

Alex, taking a swig of his Bud Light, said, "Sorry to hear about your wife." Swallowing the beer, he said, "That must be tough."

The shorter boy, his lips pursed, nodded his head

in agreement.

And Jeffrey, squinting his eyes as the sun's rays entered into the car from the windshield, said, "I appreciate it." Raising his beer bottle, inciting a semi-toast, he said, "I'm sorry for giving you and your friends shit that time in the garage." Alex and the shorter boy raised their bottles. Jeffrey, his hand still in the air in front of him, said, "You guys were just being kids. I had no right."

The sun rose higher into the sky. The darkness turning into dawn.

The three clanked their bottles together, sitting back to watch the sun brighten the atmosphere.

Jeffrey, leaning back into his seat, said, "Truce?"

"Truce," Alex said.

Drama Dolls

Monday:

SPANNING HALF THE DINER'S front was a large window. Through it, William could be seen drinking coffee. He sat alone, an empty spot in front of him. A spot set with a napkin, fork and spoon, and upside down coffee cup.

He checked his watch and then looked at Jeffrey through the glare as he entered the establishment. Around the diner, patrons ate eggs, bacon, and toast. Drinking orange juice while engaging in conversation. There were chicken fried steaks on hot plates. Hash browns with shredded cheese burnt on top. Some customers had hot coffee in mugs. Families, they got together for a morning tradition.

Mounted on brackets were flat screen televisions. Broadcasting throughout the breakfast joint was the local newscast. A news anchor threw the newscast over to the weatherman, who was standing in front of the map of the local area.

He was telling the viewers that the next several days would be dry and sunny. "So, if you're thinking about heading to the pool, the entire week looks perfect," the meteorologist said. "Later on, I'll have your seven day forecast."

A waitress working a section with no empty tables, she carried breakfast dishes on her serving tray. She dropped the meals to various customers, receiving smiles as her tray lightened with each step. Meandering toward William and Jeffrey's area, she flipped her tiny notepad for a clear space.

Rushed, sitting opposite of William, Jeffrey quickly flipped over his coffee cup. The server asked the new diner what he wanted to drink. "Coffee," Jeffrey said. "I definitely need coffee." She nodded without looking at him. Getting situated, sinking into the booth's cushion, Jeffrey made himself comfortable.

William eyed his counterpart with a curious expression. His eyebrows lowered. Taking a quick look

Drama Dolls

around the diner to make sure no one was staring, William's attention returned to Jeffrey.

A thick coat of Russian Red lip gloss was splattered across Jeffrey's lips. Pale pink blush over a warm foundation that hid his imperfections, it was evenly spread across Jeffrey's cheeks. His hair combed back behind his ears, you could see the outline of foundation around Jeffrey's hair line.

"Sorry I'm late," he said.

Sipping his cup, avoiding Jeffrey's gaze, William stared in his direction. He stared through his friend. Jeffrey's expression was blank. "You look like shit," William said. "You OK?"

When the news program returned from commercial, the anchor teased a story about a break-in. Jeffrey slapped William's hand and then listened in on the newscast. His neck turned sharply to the television, but soon after, Jeffrey's head returned to William to reduce the invisible stares on the burglars.

Irritated with the slap, William returned the favor, lightly tapping the top of Jeffrey's knuckles.

Enlarging his eyes, inconspicuously motioning to the television with his neck, Jeffrey whispered, "Listen."

The anchor was saying how a late night break-in resulted in many valuables being stolen from a local house.

The owner of the house, Melissa Pierce, said that most of the items taken were valuables from her grandmother. "I can't believe someone would steal this stuff," she said into the camera. Framed in the left center of the screen, she said, "These items mean nothing to them but a great deal to my family." She began to cry and then the camera cut back to the anchor in the studio.

Approaching the pair of Dolls with a carafe in one hand, the waitress, her lips curled to hold in a smile, cheeks with half dimples, poured the hot drink into Jeffrey's cup. A trembling hand, the coffee an unsteady stream, the server nearly overfilled the mug.

"Are you going to eat?" she said to Jeffrey. Her voice high and melodic, she was holding in a laugh. Her customer waving her off, the server moved on. Hitting her thigh against the table, she excused herself, slowly receding into the kitchen. A din of faint laughter erupted in the distance.

"Did you hear that?" Jeffrey said.

"Hear what?"

Above them, coming from the television, the anchor was saying that if you have any information on the burglary to contact your local police department.

Surprised at the calmness of William, Jeffrey threw up his hands, palms out in the air.

Drama Dolls

"What? That?"

Jeffrey nodded his head up and down in a rapid pace. He drank his coffee, his eyes still staring into William's with anxiousness.

William, cupping his glass with his hand, he said, "I don't think the police will find the burglars." Calm in his demeanor, he shrugged languidly.

Slightly worried about the newscast, but relieved that William was not exhibiting any worry whatsoever, Jeffrey drank his coffee. Holding the glass up to his mouth, his eyes panning left to right, he said, "I haven't slept."

Watching the door to the kitchen swing, William said, "I can tell."

William was blurry in this state. Rubbing his eyes, Jeffrey said, "Do I have bags?"

Shaking his head slowly, the cup of coffee in hand, William said, "No."

The long night before hit Jeffrey's aging body like a train. It could have possibly been the marijuana and alcohol, but staying up all night without sleep had to contribute as well. The previous nights, he had seen a few hours of rest, but gradually, the sleep had become scarce. Jeffrey's eyes were tired. His eyelids were drooping by the second.

Sniffing, William said, "You smell like pot, dude."

Smelling his armpits, first the right and then the left, Jeffrey shrugged. "Not sure why." Inhaling his pit again, right arm straight up to the ceiling, the sleep deprived Jeffrey said, "I don't smell anything."

The voice, irritated and crabby, it said, "Everybody's on to you."

William, his mouth curled downward, frustrated with his friend, said, "Smell again." Provoking Jeffrey, William said, "Seriously. You smell like pot."

Crinkling his nose, Jeffrey sniffed from his right shoulder, down his arm, around the front part of his waist, up his chest, and then down his entire left side. He inhaled deeply, closing his eyes to relish in his entire stink of a frame. Holding in his body's aroma, Jeffrey eventually exhaled through his nose until his body deflated. Opening his eyes, he said, "Nope. Don't smell anything."

William rolled his eyes and then looked out into the diner.

Aside from Lena, William was Jeffrey's only real friend. After She had passed, his free time had increased dramatically. All the extra hours translated into reverting

Drama Dolls

back to old habits. Days of sleeping became days of drinking became days of online surfing. He scoured porno sites. All sorts. A month long trial period led to downloading photos and videos on his hard drive. There were pop-up windows for other sites that whet his appetite. Other services. Jeffrey, he searched for adult toys the shape of film star vaginas.

William, conversely, was part of a virtual club. A fetish site. Dressing up in women's clothing and chatting online via webcam. Free trial just for signing up.

Discovering the fetish site through random searches, Jeffrey had set up an account, logging him in to a whole new life. Since he was dealing with the pain of his past existence, a brand spanking new reality was appealing.

Before the night could turn to day, Jeffrey found himself ordering outfits from websites specializing in women's attire. He purchased from sites that William shared. The sites, they appeared on Jeffrey's screen as he clicked the hyperlinks. On the web storefronts were outfits ranging from office workers to nurses to cheerleaders to nuns.

Soon, Jeffrey's credit card statement was showing hundreds of dollars in women's clothing. Momentarily, his credit card statement was showing hundreds of dollars in adult videos and sex toys. Concealed, unmarked boxes appearing on his front door step each week, Jeffrey's life without Her was beginning.

"This just in," the anchor said on the television. "The break-in has been solved." Jeffrey's head jerked up to the program. "Police officials say the burglars were local kids in the area looking for presents for their parents." Footage of the neighborhood was shown on the screen. Random shots of street signs nearby, houses in the area, and police officers circled in a group. When the videotape ran its course, the anchor returned on camera. "The owner said she feels sorry for the kids and hopes they learn their lesson that robbing from a person to help out another is not right."

The camera zoomed out to include the weatherman, who was now sitting next to the anchor. "Looks like we have a Robin Hood situation," the anchor said.

Laughing, the weatherman said, "Yeah, let's hope those kids learn a valuable lesson." Turning to the camera, the angle shot zooming in on his face, the meteorologist said, "Now, going from Robin Hood to *your* neighborhood, but what can I say but the weather for the

Drama Dolls

foreseeable future will be absolutely fabulous."

Jeffrey's shoulders sank. He stared at the broadcast until it went into commercials.

William, reeling Jeffrey back into reality, said in a haughty tone, "Are you sure you don't smell anything?" He raised his cup to his mouth.

And Jeffrey, losing interest in the television altogether, said, "I also haven't had a chance to shower yet."

The mug's rim covering his face, William did his best to avoid eye contact. There was a spoon nearby hitting a plate. A baby crying in the distance. The restroom door closing and then latching. Whatever they were, William noticed the distractions. Every distraction.

Each waitress who emerged from the kitchen, William could tell what the order was on her tray. A stack of pancakes with blueberry syrup caught his eyes. A bowl of fruit on the side of a Denver omelet. Anything held his attention.

The heavyset customer in the tan suit with his tie loosened, William counted a third orange juice. A second helping of pancakes, empty butter containers on the edge of the table, the Drama Doll took note.

Glancing over the entire restaurant, his attention coming to, William said, "You really need to get some sleep."

Before Jeffrey could answer, William turned his head and watched a mother care for her infant child. She picked him up from his booster seat in order to wipe his face. The little boy squirmed, his head moving left to right to avoid the washcloth. Fighting with her son, the mother held his chin with her free hand, scrubbing with the other. The boy winced, his eyes closed. "Stay still," the mother said.

"Not after this coffee," Jeffrey said, holding up the glass. Sipping the drink, the warmth tickled his throat. The stares around the diner were harsh. Heaviness upon him. The two of them, so much to say when dressed up as Drama Dolls, the regular old men could not hold a conversation.

The voice of sarcastic reason, it was paranoid. It said, "Everybody's looking at us."

Finally, William, he said, "What time is, uh, Lena coming?" He swallowed.

Jeffrey opened his mouth to speak. But then, Lena entered the establishment. Sliding in next to Jeffrey, her tiny waist touching his, Lena said, "Lipstick looks great."

Jeffrey and Lena flashed their teeth to each other. Wide smiles. "Thanks," Jeffrey said. He said, "William didn't notice."

Drama Dolls

Lena cut William a disdainful look.

Mimicking her, Jeffrey sneered at him too.

William, his eyes bouncing from Jeffrey to Lena's and then back, said, "Staying in character?"

Without a second thought, Jeffrey said, "Just getting ready for tonight."

A family of six entered. They waited at the front of the diner to be seated. Lined up in a row from tallest to shortest, the father asked for a menu. The waitress assigned to the Drama Dolls' table, she was dishing out a menu to both mother and father.

"We just need to clean off a table," she said. Then she swung around the half wall dividing the main room and pay station and collected a five dollar bill that was slid under a plate at a table covered in dirty dishes.

Assisting the busboy, who was collecting plates into a bin, the server wiped down the tablecloth and pushed in the table's chairs.

After a condescending glare toward Lena, William said, "Oh, we're doing that?"

Lena sat with a muted expression. Her eyes went wide. She smiled with her teeth, her actual face a replica of her mask face.

Cup in hand, moist lips stained along the rim, slurping the coffee into his mouth, Jeffrey said, "Totally."

103

Waving the family members to their seats, the waitress said, "I'll be right with you to take your orders."

As the family passed the cheerleaders' table, the siblings displayed a montage of stares, giggling, and an "Oh my God!" The mother, catching wind of the sight, pulled her youngest in close to her and said, "Shhh!" When the boy continued to laugh, his mother cupped his mouth with her palm.

The server, she swung around Lena, took her order, and then disappeared into the kitchen.

Echoing what Jeffrey replied, Lena said, "Totally."

Checking the time, Jeffrey, he said, "After breakfast we've got an appointment."

Walking through the house, the assistant was always one or two rooms ahead. Picking up clothes or kicking shoes under the bed, she scrambled last minute in order to show the room's full beauty. Straightening curtains, wiping off dust with her finger, the assistant put in place anything that jumped out at her.

A vacation photo was in the guest bedroom. A smiling couple in the center. The assistant grabbed the photo and shoved it into a dresser drawer. Scanning the

Drama Dolls

bedroom one last time, she fluffed the pillows on the bed. Nodding her head, the assistant smiled in approval. Before leaving, the assistant, she closed the room's door. This was her signal that the room was ready for viewing.

The house had been on the market through spring and summer. Price declines indicated by the REDUCED PRICE sign in the front yard. Overgrown grass being cut sporadically. Neighborhood kids' candy wrappers lost in the lawn. A few cigarette butts were scattered on the sidewalk. There were fast food cups filled with rain water. A cellophane burger wrapper crumpled into a ball. Any piece of litter from drivers passing by called the yard home.

Royal Wedding Hostas ran up the staircase of the front steps. Weeds in between waiting to be pulled. Tulips were in the flower bed in front of the banister. Peppered in the flower arrangement were Hosta White Feathers. More weeds.

The realtor gave the nickel and dime tour, allowing William, Jeffrey, and Lena to self-guide and familiarize themselves with the nuances of the Queen Anne. There were high ceilings, ornate woodwork, and a brick fireplace that stood out upon entering.

"Any kids?" Jane said. The realtor asked because of all the space the house offered. She could determine how serious a buyer was by discovery questions.

Lena, her arm through Jeffrey's, shook her head. Smiling, she said, "Nope. Just me and my husband."

Continuing with her line of questioning, the realtor, she said, "This is a lot of room for just the two of you." A serious tone, she said, "Do you plan on having children?" Observing their reactions was something Jane did with all her showings.

Admiring the decorative staircase from afar, each spindle carved with the same design, Lena just shook her head. Smiling, leading Jeffrey through the old house, she was pulling him closer as she turned each corner.

"This is sooo pretty," she said. Turning to address her proposed husband, Lena said, "Don't you think?" The accidental bride rubbed her hand up and down Jeffrey's arm. Playing the part, she said, "Honey?"

Jeffrey, he nodded, surveying the place with each glance.

The library off the living room was a quaint sitting and reading area. Bookshelves up and down the walls, they covered the mass of the wall space, giving new owners plenty of room for Dickens, Poe, and Twain classics. Built-in shelves in the walls were adjacent to the dining room. There were custom designed bookstands around the perimeter.

Drama Dolls

One large bay window covered the wall that joined the home's interior and exterior. A vintage desk with curved wood, detailed to impress admirers, was in front of the window. Facing outdoors, the drawer hardware was shiny brass. Every knob was exactly the same.

Lena, her mouth dropping open, pulled out a drawer. A dusting of wood fell to the hardwood. "How gorgeous," she said, turning to Jeffrey. "This would make a great office desk."

Outside the window was an empty field of grass. Opposite the field was another small neighborhood of old homes. Houses from a different era. Just above the roofs of the antique dwellings was a tree line.

Nudging the groom in the elbow, getting his attention, Lena said, "Sitting in front of the window as you get your work done."

Agreeing without ever taking a look, Jeffrey said, "Yes, dear." His eyes were past the point of burning. Glossy and empty, Jeffrey blinked repeatedly. Getting his tenth wind was his saving grace for looking interested.

"Oh?" the realtor said. "What type of work are you in?" The real estate agent followed Jeffrey with her eyes as he paced around the room.

"My husband acquires valuables. Mainly jewelry,"

Lena said.

Engaged, wanting to keep the communication moving, the realtor said, "Oh. Well, the owners were big fans of antiques. This desk actually came from Europe."

"Oooh. Europe. Did you hear that, honey?"

Appraising the desk, the baroque corners caught Jeffrey's attention. Falling in and out of a fog, he said, "*Were* fans?"

Dishing out a disconcerted look to Lena, the realtor said, "There's only one owner now."

Twirling toward the dining area, Lena stopped short. "Oh my God!" Her voice, becoming higher with each syllable, ended in a squeal. Staring her in the face was a wooden table the size of a compact car. "Jeffrey, look at the dining room table." Her stomach sucking in, her chest out, a stationary smile with her mouth open, Lena was beside herself.

The realtor grinned. "Everyone who has looked at the house has had the same reaction."

Curious, Lena said, "How many people have come through?"

Jane placed her finger on her squeezed lips. Eyes closed together, eyebrows furrowing, she said, "There's been a good amount. Four, maybe?"

Jeffrey acknowledged the realtor and then

Drama Dolls

continued to scope out the house.

The table's fringe was handcrafted. Rounded slits along the edges. There was elaborate detail running along the border in between the slits. The sturdy tree trunks for legs looked like upside down bowling pins with smooth, flat bottoms. Thin ankles expanding into massive thighs that were screwed in forcefully into the bottom of the table's top. Each chair matching the table's hand-cut pattern, the seating could accommodate a fielded baseball team with designated hitter.

Enthralled with the owner's taste, Jeffrey said, "Impressive."

Lena, repeating the information to Jeffrey, said, "Did you hear that? Four people have already looked at the house." She searched for a response but got nothing.

"This is a beautiful home," the realtor said. "It won't be on the market too long."

Along the wall was a buffet. A similar design to the table, all the dining room furniture looked like it came in a set. Complementing the hardwood floor, the cheerful deep red walls ran the course of the dining area. This was the only room on the main floor that was not painted a creamy yellow.

"Nice color," Jeffrey said.

His inner voice, salivating at the furniture, it had

an emotional erection.

Noise above them, footsteps moving across the ceiling, caused Jeffrey to look up. The thumping triggered the crystal chandelier to shake. Made from a variety of different crystals, the light fixture was a nice addition to the room. Manufactured from glass and crystal prisms, any light that struck the chandelier was both reflected and refracted. "Imagine the dinner parties we could have," Lena said. She was very convincing, almost forgetting the reason for their desire to view.

Open houses equaled open doors. Scoping out upcoming targets to burgle became easy. This time of year made selling homes favorable. From the length of the lawn, Jeffrey knew the owner wasn't around much. The owner wasn't invested anymore.

A built-in china cabinet was directly across the buffet. Inside, the cabinet was filled with Cambridge Rose Point crystal and glassware. Unique pieces such as vases, relish dishes, French dressing bottles, they were all etched with the Rose Point design. There were cruet sets, candy boxes, and comports, enough crystal to astound any guest.

Lena stood in awe of the collection of antique dinnerware. "I can't believe how beautiful this stuff is," she said. "I couldn't even imagine serving food with these pieces."

Drama Dolls

"As I said, the owners were very much into collecting," Jane said. Gaining Jeffrey's attention, she said, "Are you a collector as well?"

"I guess you could say that," Jeffrey said.

Rejoining Jeffrey, grabbing his hand, Lena said, "Jeffrey knows a lot about antiques. Don't you honey?"

Footsteps up above moved across the ceiling. The swinging chandelier starting up again.

"Are you familiar with these pieces?" the realtor said.

Jeffrey, recalling the history of the Cambridge Glass company, said, "Although the Cambridge Class company was around since the early nineteen hundreds, the Rose Point etching didn't come into production until nineteen-thirty."

Leaning into the glass, noting the valuable crystal, Jeffrey said that Rose Point was so extraordinary because it succeeded during the Great Depression. "Think about that for a second," Jeffrey said. On a roll, tiredness not even an issue, he said, "The stock market crashed in October nineteen-twenty-nine. Black Tuesday. The market lost fourteen billion dollars that day alone."

Confidence rising, he said, "Imagine how much confidence you have in your product that you roll out a line of crystal, of all things."

Fascinated by the knowledge Jeffrey had stored in his brain, Jane and Lena glanced at one another.

The voice of impressive reason, it said, "Interesting."

"May I?" Jeffrey said. The realtor nodding, he opened the china hutch and pulled out a crystal glass.

The glassware was just as dazzling. Water goblets for an entire dinner party, some were clear while others were pressed glasses. "Feel how thin this is," Jeffrey said.

Extending her arm out, Lena carefully rubbed her fingers around the perimeter. Tracing her thumb around the glass's outside, she said, "It even feels expensive."

"Each piece of glass was priced at around twenty dollars. Some of the dishes could draw up to three hundred," Jeffrey said.

Hearing the prices, Lena quickly withdrew her fingers from the crystal.

Jeffrey returned the glass to the cabinet's shelf and closed the door.

Lined up against the walls in each room were boxes packed for moving. Different sized ones, marked with a permanent marker to distinguish rooms. Some read FRAGILE – DISHES. Others indicated clothing, shoes, and things to donate. The tape coming off the ends, curling into each other, you could tell that the cartons had

Drama Dolls

been sitting for a while.

Walking toward the swinging door that separated the dining room from the kitchen, the realtor stalled. Her hand on the door, ready to push, building to suspense, she said, "I know you loved the glassware but are you ready to see the kitchen?"

Pushing open the wooden door, the realtor said, "I give you the modern kitchen for the Victorian home."

The remodeled kitchen, modernized for mass appeal, drove Lena into a state of excitement. A Wolf oven with six burners, stainless steel exterior, it had a temperature max of five hundred degrees. "This is a commercial oven designed for residential use," Jane said. "So, it's kind of like what you see in the restaurants but not as powerful."

Placed in the middle of the longest wall, the setup was ideal for cooking. Counter space extending on each side, a stand up pantry, and in the center, there was an island by itself, a prep station with its own faucet and sink.

Glass cabinets above the counters, which ran the course of two walls, they were filled with wine tumblers, designer plates, and glasses that were displayed for guests to see.

Shaking her head, her heartbeat in a tizzy, Lena said, "Wow. Everything is displayed so nicely."

Flabbergasted and overwhelmed, she said, "They really did like to entertain."

In the corner near the pantry was an Ascend commercial refrigerator. Stainless steel to match the oven, the fridge had four bays, three for refrigeration and one for freezing. On the top of the fridge-freezer were distinct digital meters for controlling the food's temperature.

Kitchen walls made of Venetian plaster were emphasized with decorative scratch marks to give a soft intonation and informal feel. The wall colors alternated from a burnt orange to an aureolin yellow. "It looks like something you'd find in an Italian villa," Lena said. Captivated by the room, Lena almost fainted. Fanning herself with her hand, she said, "Is it hot in here?"

"Lovely, isn't it?" the real estate agent said.

"Beautiful," Jeffrey said. "Totally."

In the alcove, a separate nook that was an extension of the kitchen, was a powder room.

Lena, highly emotional, she said, "Baby, there's a bathroom in here too." Walking in, the half-bath complemented the kitchen's design. A glass chandelier matching the kitchen's lighting, the powder room had a European styled sink and vanity combo. "What a beautiful place," Lena said. Feeling the wall with her palm, she said, "What color is this?"

Drama Dolls

Leaning in close, the realtor said, "I think it's salmon."

Standing in front of the staircase to the second floor, William appeared suddenly, having broken away when the group first entered. The commission-based salesperson smiled. "What do you think?"

A glazed expression, William said, "It's nice."

Jane, addressing her clients, said, "Any questions so far?"

Lena stood with a blank stare. Jeffrey was staring up the staircase. And William, he was sweating.

Spinning toward the staircase, looking upward to the second story, the realtor said, "Well, let's see the upstairs."

In a row, the train of people paraded up the flight of steps. Combined, the first and second floor were almost the height of three normal stories. Walking up, their necks were falling back in order to see the ceiling. Separating the landing where the stairs turned sharply right was a vertical window with stained glass. The way the sun hit the glass made for a colorful kaleidoscope.

"This is so breathtaking," Lena said. She stood for a second to bask in the rainbow of colors shining on her. Closing her eyes, taking in the sun that was filtering through, a smile formed on her face.

The smallest guest bedroom kept much of the design consistent with the main floor. William looked up at the woodwork. The crown molding along the high ceilings was painted to match the trim. Fresh white highlighting pea-green walls was a nice touch. White trim alongside the windows, the sun shining into the house offered natural light.

"I love the radiators," Lena said. The hot water heat pushed out of standing registers in the corner of each room. Painted a glossy silver. The owners were meticulous with their property. Pulled out prior to use, the registers had been sandblasted, primed, and then painted.

Nodding in agreement, the realtor, she said, "Yes! Usually with old homes like this the radiators have layers and layers of paint." She walked over to the heating source and traced her finger down halfway. "They spent a lot of their time making this house beautiful."

Cutting a look toward Jeffrey, the realtor closed her eyes and smiled.

Agreeing with the agent, Lena, she said, "It's gorgeous."

Glancing around the room one last time, the group exited into the hallway.

Walking past a closed door, Lena said, "Can we go in there?"

Drama Dolls

The realtor, shaking her head, said, "No. That room is the master bedroom. The owner requests that it not be shown." Locking stares with all three of the guests, apologizing non-verbally with her eyes, she said, "The owner does promise that the room will fully meet all expectations."

An open door next to the master was another bedroom. Throwing out information before entering, Jane said, "This room is actually larger than the master. It was used as a sitting room because it has a fireplace."

When the undercover Dolls entered, Lena stopped short at the white bricked fireplace in the center of the back wall. Positioned in front of the fireplace was a pair of matching Victorian button back parlor chairs. The bloody red chairs surrounded a white marble-top table stand.

"This looks so elegant," Lena said. She slid around one of the chairs and sat down. Hard on her buttocks, she said, "They're not very comfortable." Lena leaned her head back so she could see the ceiling. Along it was the same crown molding found in the rest of the rooms on the floor.

A large circular area rug covered much of the floor space. Twisting her waist, looking down at the matching red-colored carpet piece, Lena's attention was drawn to the furniture on either side. "How did I miss the fancy couches?" On either side of the rug were golden yellow upholstered Victorian couches.

The inner voice of arrogant reason said, "Go ahead. Drop some knowledge on her."

"These are actually called fainting chairs," Jeffrey said.

Behind him, mocking him in a little child's voice, William muttered under his breath, "Dees are cowed feenting cheers."

"The theory was that a woman's corset was so tight that she literally fainted from the lack of air."

Ignoring William's antics, Lena said, "You're so smart." She cut a look to William and squinted her eyes in disgust. Then she turned to Jeffrey and said, "I'm so glad I married you."

Picking up on the tension, the real estate agent said, "Are we ready to see the bathroom?"

The bathroom was a classic design. Subway tiles, black with white grout, traversed the room's walls. The shower surround was a modern-day claw foot tub design without feet that rested square on the floor tiles. Octagon tiles under their feet, they were heated for the winter's cold nights.

About eye level, a white wood trim disrupted the

Drama Dolls

dark tiles in order to break up the pattern. Lena, standing in front of the pedestal sink, said, "I love these old bathrooms." Her eyes turned toward the toilet seat. A water line and electrical cord shot out from underneath. The seat offered a remote control. She said, "What is that?"

And Jane, hovering over their shoulders, taking her own peek, said, "It's a bidet." Lena turned to address the realtor. Jeffrey stood still, unfazed. "The owners fell in love with the bidets overseas. It was a must have," the agent said.

Jane spun her body around to engage William. The two had a brief stare down. William said, "Nice house."

"That's so cool," Lena said. She glanced at William and caught him rolling his eyes. "I love how eccentric they were." Lena, she said, "These types of people would *never* give me the time of day."

Breaking up the tedium, Jeffrey said, "You mentioned there is only one owner now." Jane nodded, agreeing to his statement. "Where is—"

Coming down from the attic, interrupting the milieu, the assistant smiled while nodding her head.

All turning toward the assistant simultaneously, Jane said, "Yes, well…" Changing the subject, she said,

119

"Would you like to see the attic?"

Jaunting up yet another staircase, the group members found themselves inside a finished studio room. Wooden bookshelves along the perimeter enclosed the large area. Filing cabinets and computer equipment filled one corner. There was a futon in another. In the middle of the room was a leather sectional in front of a television stand.

There were dormer windows on each side. A single closet in the corner. A small walk-in was used for random pieces of clothing. Some were forgotten, some a size too large. Other clothes bought at a rummage sale.

"This attic was used as a lounge," the assistant said.

William sighed, his gaze finding Lena's. He checked his watch and then looked around the open quarter.

Listening to only fragments of the realtor's pitch, each item was inventoried in Jeffrey's mind for future reference.

In the dining room, aside from the crystal, the china hutch held decorative silverware and chrome-plated platters. Antique tea cups with matching kettles. Butter dishes, steins, pitchers, a corresponding set of dinnerware.

"Don't forget the packed boxes," the voice of

Drama Dolls

anxious reason said.

Period furniture throughout the house was inventoried. Jeffrey noticed there were casters on each dresser and vanity. Certain pieces featured designs on the front drawers, some with carved faces and others with lions.

Outside the burglaries, the only other time Jeffrey had inventoried his possessions was when She was still alive. When they had first married, the couple had shared a charming one bedroom apartment across town. Both of them finishing school, working a pair of part-time jobs outside of studying, Jeffrey and the Missus had envisioned buying a historical house.

The beginning years of their marriage, planning for a home similar to the kinds the Drama Dolls burgled, Jeffrey and his wife would venture out to estate sales and antique stores in the surrounding areas and acquire old paintings and used furniture they could restore.

Dropping them into spaces in the apartment did not leave room for traditional pieces, so the newlyweds' furniture, end tables, and the like looked as if they were zapped in from the past.

An alternate universe consuming their residence. Their lives.

The insurance agent laughing when Jeffrey and his wife came in for renter's insurance, he said, "I don't know what this stuff is actually worth, but I'm glad you thought about insuring your possessions."

Inventorying the antique furniture was an exercise of fruition. An exercise Jeffrey was finally getting to use.

Standing in the center of the attic, the house's highest peak, Jane said, "This home offers a lot of room for storage and living." Finishing up her spiel, she said, "It *really* is a beautiful house." Lingering around for any last questions or requests, the realtor checked the time.

The group had been touring the house for nearly two hours. William, standing off to the side, looked out the dormer. Their position in the house was high above the ground. Looking straight out ahead, off into the distance of reality, William could see a small wooded area. The tops of the trees reminded him of his pom-poms' feathers.

Grabbing ahold of Jeffrey's hand, cupping it into her palm, Lena said, "Honey, what do you think of the house?"

Drama Dolls

Pirouetting to see the attic as a whole, Jeffrey said, "I love it. It's definitely something I could see myself in."

Exiting the house, Jeffrey walked down the front steps to the curb. Just short of the boulevard, he turned around to capture the mammoth sized structure in one mental photograph. The curtain in the master bedroom window was partially open. The outline of old-fashioned pieces in view, Jeffrey envisioned the house's schematic.

His gaze working side to side, each room's floor plan memorized, Jeffrey stayed quiet and to himself.

"Tonight we will rob this house," the inner Jeffrey said.

Standing on the front porch, the realtor and assistant talked to William and Lena. The assistant, she was locking the door behind her, returning the key to the box on the door handle.

In the middle of a semi-circle crowding the front entrance, Jane, standing with her hands on her hips, said, "What do you think is going through his head?" The small group looked down toward Jeffrey, whose attention was absorbing the house's detail.

William and Lena, they both shrugged simultaneously. They both knew this was a formality.

123

Something the burglars had done many times before.

Pulling on the key box to ensure it was secure, Jane turned to William. "Can't say this was a complete loss then," she said. Unzipping her purse, pulling out her sunglasses, the realtor said, "Is he wearing makeup?"

Nodding slowly, William said, "Totally."

Jeffrey, Barb, and Lena watched the realtor and her assistant vacate the grounds. Grass as high as the FOR SALE sign, kicking weeds in front of his feet, Jeffrey said, "We've got time. Who wants to go to a baseball game?"

William, looking down into the grass, said, "I'll pass."

"C'mon," Jeffrey said, kneeling down to pull weeds in sight. "We got like four hours until dark." Pulling out a handful of dandelions and annual sow thistles, Jeffrey tossed them aside.

Short in his response, his eyes looking anywhere but at Jeffrey's, William said, "I'm good."

Jumping in to support Jeffrey, Lena said, "Don't be a fun killer. It'll be great." She stared at William, her eyes widening. She flipped her hand into his chest until she caught his attention.

William, looking up toward Lena, then to a kneeling Jeffrey, said, "Dude, you need to get some sleep."

Drama Dolls

Repaying the harsh stare to Lena, and then rounding back to the captain of the cheerleader gang, he said, "Get some sleep. We'll meet back up later. K?"

"William," Jeffrey said, a pile of dandelions next to him. Throwing down the batch of weeds that were in his hand, he said, stretching out the word, "Will-Lee."

Standing still, no movement whatsoever, William glanced to the ground before him, his attention focused on an anthill in the sidewalk crack. Sliding the bottom of his shoe over the hill, leveling off the dirt, he said nothing. Ants, they were running in every direction.

"You're a poopy head," Lena said.

"Willster." Singing the word, Jeffrey said, "Willinator." The heat was making his face itch. Sucking in his lips, spreading out the lipstick to make it even, he said, "I'm gonna ask one more time. Who wants to go to a baseball game?" Standing to his feet, face to face with William, Jeffrey waited for a response. His body tightening, his fists clenching.

William sharply looked up, his eyebrows lowering slowly, lips tightened, and teeth clenched so hard they hurt, he said, "I'll. See. You. Tonight." He walked around the front of his car. Eying Jeffrey the entire time, William started the vehicle and drove away.

Witnessing the scene unfold, and not wanting the

situation to escalate, Lena said, "I guess it's just us." Her arm swung around Jeffrey's waist. Pulling him close to her, she leaned her head into his shoulder. Eyes shut, a closed smile, she said, "Your car or mine?"

Jeffrey, being dragged farther away from the pile of weeds, craned his head back to the sidewalk. "OK," Lena said. "We'll take the 'Vette." Releasing her hand, Lena continued.

Walking toward the car, the distance between her and Jeffrey grew noticeably. She turned to her groom cheerleader and said, "Jeffrey?"

Running back to the weeds, Jeffrey kneeled down and collected the miscellaneous dandelions and sow thistles. "Just let me throw these away real quick."

The minor league ball stadium was half-filled with spectators. A middle of the day, Monday game hardly drew the crowd the stadium wanted.

Cars were sprinkled in parking spots outside the baseball diamond, some in rows to themselves. The lot was as big as the field was wide. Spanning an entire block, the stadium could accommodate nearly one thousand cars. On this day, though, there was only a quarter of that amount.

Pulling through a row of yellow painted lines, the

Drama Dolls

farthest from the stadium, Jeffrey angled into the last spot of the corresponding row. The Corvette's nose facing the concrete base of the streetlight, the car idled crookedly over the yellow lines that were now crisscrossed under the tires.

Lena stuck her head out of the window and looked down. "I don't think you're straight," she said. Peering directly ahead of her, taillights of sedans in her face, she said, "I don't think I should be able to read bumper stickers looking out the passenger window."

Jeffrey shifted into park and turned off the engine. Snapping at Lena, his temper short, he said, "I think we're fine!" As Jeffrey opened the door to climb out, he noticed the female Drama Doll was motionless.

The voice of annoyed reason said, "I think she's pee-issed!"

Leaning through the window, his upper body in the driver's seat, Jeffrey said, "I'm sorry for snapping at you." Lena slowly turned to address him. "I'm just upset that William didn't come. Please come to the game with me." Her lips the shape of a fingernail, twisting downward slowly, Lena reached for the door handle. "I promise I won't be a poopy head anymore," Jeffrey said.

Lena chuckled, her teeth starting to show as a smile formed on her face. She said, "William's a poopy

Jason Tanamor

head. You're a poopy face." She looked at Jeffrey and stuck out her tongue.

Walking to the entrance, the sun at its hottest, Jeffrey's face was tingling from the makeup splashed across him. He said, "This is so exciting. I can't wait." Sweat building around his nostrils, Jeffrey's nose started to itch. Rotating his mouth in a clockwise motion to no avail, he finally scratched the tip of his nose with his finger.

Music blasted from the stadium. Spilling out into the parking lot, Jeffrey and Lena began to shimmy as they trotted toward the entrance. A selection of dance music and disco hits revved up the crowd. Over the speaker, the announcer said, "What a beautiful day for a baseball game."

Jeffrey and Lena looked at each other. Together, they said, "Totally." Their pace increasing to a jog, the pair ran the rest of the way.

His skin itching from the makeup, Jeffrey scrunched his face for relief. Sweat falling down his nose, the makeup beginning to smear, Jeffrey rubbed his nose on his sleeve.

The couple approached the ticket booth. Pulling out his wallet, Jeffrey grabbed a twenty dollar bill. Holding up two fingers, the employee behind the window looked up, smiled, and then looked back down. The smile

Drama Dolls

growing, the boy slid a pair of tickets under the window slot.

"Sixteen dollars," he said. Grabbing four singles from the register, the boy slid the change to Jeffrey. Avoiding eye contact, his mouth now open and in full smirk, he said, "Thank you, ma'am. Enjoy the game." Then he laughed and walked away from the window.

The section that Jeffrey and Lena were sitting in was scarcely populated. An elderly couple behind them sat and watched, holding hands as the visiting team's catcher popped the ball into the outfield. The ball grew bigger after it exploded off the bat. The older man, his socks pulled up to his knees, released his grip and clapped as the centerfielder made a diving catch. His wife, eating popcorn, stared as the home team ran into the dugout.

While the teams were switching between innings, a team of employees ran onto the field with handheld T-shirt guns. Able to launch shirts into the bleachers, a girl working the apparatus pointed the barrel toward Jeffrey and Lena's section.

Lena stood up to her feet and waved her hand. "I want a shirt," she said. Jumping up and down, her arm swinging left to right, Lena said, "Up here!"

The announcer over the speaker system said,

"Who wants some T-shirts?" There were pockets of applause around the stands. Lena jumped higher up and down, stretching her arm into the air. The bleacher began to shake under Jeffrey's feet. The announcer, he said, "Is everybody ready?"

Music started blasting. Lyrics from the speakers singing, *"Everybody dance now!"* The beat was filling the stands. *"Everybody dance now!"*

The announcer's voice, coming through the speakers muffled, said, "And launch!"

The girl working the shirt launcher fired the shirts toward the Dolls' section. The first one stopped short, landing in an empty row. Jeffrey saw a preadolescent boy run from his seat to retrieve it.

Bass pumping through the system, shirts now launching repeatedly, the crowd was getting into it. Lena, bouncing higher and higher, watched as a shirt flew over her head. Clapping, she screamed down to the firing squad. "Up here!"

In the outfield, warming up their arms, the opposing team's centerfielder played catch with the right fielder. As the shirts flew into the stadium seats, the rest of the visiting team's players made their way onto the field.

Disappointed, slightly pouting, Lena sat back down next to Jeffrey. She was sweating profusely. Wiping

Drama Dolls

her hand across her forehead, she pulled her hair back into a ponytail.

Jeffrey patted her thigh, indirectly telling her that she had given a valiant effort.

The music overhead, it played, *"Everybody dance now…"* and then cut short.

Lena's eyes moved toward Jeffrey, her face still forward. A smile building inside, she clapped her hands when the batter approached the plate.

Resting his palm on Lena's thigh, Jeffrey enjoyed the game from his seat.

The announcer, over the loud speaker, said, "Leading off the bottom of the third is the first baseman, Manny Valens." The crowd cheered. Valens had been sent down from the majors to rehab his knee. Slowly he was healing and was close to returning back to the St. Louis Cardinals' roster.

In front of Jeffrey and Lena was a group of adolescent boys wearing ball caps, keeping score on scorecards. One boy's dad sat at the end of the row. Lined up with their scorecards on their laps, the boys watched the game intently.

The screaming of the fans drowned out the organ that was pumping out a rally. The announcer was selling ad space for the local radio station. Once the advertisement was finished, the announcer returned to the game. "Valens' career batting average in the pros is three hundred. Today, he'll see if he can use his Major League experience against a tough up and coming pitcher from Kansas."

The pitcher threw the first pitch. Standing still, the batter let the ball pass the plate. The umpire behind home plate stood from his crouching position and called a strike. Some in attendance booed while others clapped for encouragement. The boys sitting in front of the Jeffrey and Lena marked their scorecards.

Reapplying the Russian Red, Jeffrey pursed his lips several times. Staring down over his nose, he examined his work. After he was satisfied, Jeffrey offered up the lip gloss to Lena.

She waved him off and signaled for the beer vendor. The vendor, a man wearing a tray of beer cans slung around his neck, he asked how many.

Holding up two fingers, Lena pulled out cash from her purse.

Winding up his rotation, the pitcher fired the ball down to the plate. This time, the batter swung through the pitch so hard he almost fell over. The announcer, over the speaker, said, "Strike two!" Blitzing on the big screen, an animated baseball, an angry expression in the center, became larger until it disappeared off the screen. "That

Drama Dolls

pitch was clocked at ninety two miles per hour. Talk about fast ball."

The hitter took a couple practice swings and then returned to the batter's box. Digging his front foot into the dirt, shaking his hips in rhythm, Valens focused on the pitcher.

Makeup mirror now in front of him, patting his cheeks with warm blush, Jeffrey turned his head side to side to ensure the application was even. His face covering the mirror, he kissed into it and then winked at himself.

"Eighteen dollars," the beer man said, cupping the plastic cups in his palm. Reaching out for the twenty, Lena told him to keep the tip. "Thanks! Enjoy, ladies!"

Following the beer from the vendor to Lena, a boy wearing his ball cap backward turned to face the clandestine Dolls. He started laughing, turning around quickly to avoid being seen. Nudging his friend with his elbow, the choreographed reaction resulted in each child slowly craning his neck to catch a glimpse.

The group laughed in unison.

The pitcher, leaning into the plate, stepped off the mound. Echoing throughout the stadium, the crowd booed.

The batter once again stepped out of the box and took some practice swings. The organ was playing

133

"Charge" through the speakers. Returning to the batter's box, positioning his bat behind his head, the Cardinals slugger waited for the pitch.

The kids were in a state of laughter at the sight of the colorful Jeffrey.

The pitcher stepped off the mound and released the ball from his hand. After firing the baseball, he got into a fielding position. The crowd was hushed as the ball flew down to home plate.

Baseball spinning through the air, the batter waited until the right time, calculating the distance between him and the ball, and then swung the bat.

The aluminum bat making contact with the ball made a loud sound, and at once Jeffrey and Lena stood up. The pair standing caused the boys to rise to their feet as well. Their laughter transforming to excitement, the boys' scorecards fell down off their laps. Each youngster extended his hand up in the air.

The crowd, once muted, erupted into cheers.

"And that ball, is out of here!" the announcer said.

The baseball flying toward them, the two cheerleaders extended their arms up to accommodate the height. Watching the stitches on the ball spin toward him, the white leather mixing in with red lettering and dirt spots, the homerun approached Jeffrey in dream speed.

Drama Dolls

The outfielders craning their heads, they watched the ball exit the field of play.

The ball screaming toward the Drama Dolls, Lena ducked out of the way, hiding her head behind Jeffrey's body. "Ahh," she cried, crouching down to cover herself.

Reaching out, his eyes focused on the ball, the boys jumping up and down in front of him, Jeffrey pulled the baseball down in his grasp.

Lena shrieked, her head shrunk down into her body. Her shoulders were up above her ears. The beers, still intact, were sitting on the bleacher between them. The boys in front of them were screaming. The elderly man was clapping until his hands turned red.

On the big screen, the entire stadium yelling, high fiving each other, blaring their appreciation into the field as the batter rounded the bases, was a grown man wearing a full face of makeup. Russian Red lip gloss in the center of the Jumbotron. A warm foundation covered by pale pink blush. Jeffrey's mouth wide open into a smile, holding up the ball for everyone to see.

And Lena, she was crouched behind, her ass sticking out of Jeffrey's hip. Looking like a multi-person costumed animal of some sort.

The audience, together, snickered.

Rounding the bases, hearing the roars and laughter

coming from the crowd, Manny Valens looked up at the big screen and then tripped over his cleats. Tumbling into a somersault on the dirt.

Over the speaker, the announcer, calling the game, he said, "And there's a souvenir for some sort of clown centaur-like creature."

The inner child, it was as happy as could be.

Walking back to the Corvette, flipping the ball in the air and catching it, Jeffrey held his head up in pride. A couple game goers walking by congratulated him on the catch. He smiled, held the ball up as proof, and continued on his way.

Lena walked next to him, intermittently holding his free hand and grazing his hip.

The car still a baseball diamond away, the two recounted the game. "I can't believe you caught a homerun ball," Lena said. Embarrassed about hiding behind him, she said, "I wish I got to see you catch it."

Jeffrey turned to her and put his free arm around her waist. Pulling her in close to him, he said, "Forget the game. *You* were great."

She smiled and dug her head into him.

Going with the flow, Jeffrey said, "Trust me. You didn't miss much." Leading the way as the couple headed

Drama Dolls

to the sports car, he said, "The ball was coming so fast *I* didn't even see it."

Placing her hand on his chest, the couple walked to the car. A beeping sound caught their attention. Following the sound, Jeffrey and Lena saw that a tow truck was backing in toward the Corvette.

Screaming at the top of his lungs, his gait moving from a casual walk to a jog, Jeffrey said, "Hey! That's my car." Releasing Lena from his grasp, the child at heart zoomed in on the scene. His jog became a sprint. Jeffrey dropped the baseball and bolted to the sports car. His face sweating from the sun, his nose itchy the entire sprint.

The beeping sound continued, louder and louder as Jeffrey got closer.

Lena picked up the ball off the pavement and jogged the rest of the way.

The tow truck driver, watching Jeffrey get closer, ignored the makeup-clad cheerleader and continued with his job. The slide on the tow truck was hydraulically declining down to accommodate the car. Pulling the 'Vette with a winch, the sports car began to roll toward the truck's bed.

"Didn't you hear me?" Jeffrey said. Breathing heavily, his face humid from sweat, he continued the sprint to his luxury car.

Lena, still a ways back, slowed to a powerwalk.

The tow truck driver, observing the car owner as he approached closer, strained his neck to get a better view. Seeing Jeffrey run toward him, face out of focus from the up and down motion, the truck operator started to snicker. A multi-colored face, hovering like a ghost on the indistinct Jeffrey, bouncing closer and closer to him. The snicker turned to laughter, as the makeup grew to resemble the Cheshire Cat from *Alice's Adventures in Wonderland*.

Arriving at the scene, completely exhausted, Jeffrey bent down to catch his breath. His hand on his thighs, keeled over, saliva falling onto the hot pavement, he said, "This is my car."

The Corvette, now on the truck's flatbed, was being straightened as the slide began to incline and level out. Standing upright, his heart pounding out of his chest, Jeffrey said, "Did you hear me?"

Still a couple strides back, Lena watched as Jeffrey and the tow truck driver exchanged words. Animated, pacing back and forth, his arms flailing all around, Jeffrey's facial expressions went from angry to distraught and then from crying to confused. Floundering around in a circle, body now moving in every direction, Jeffrey pulled his hair. Releasing his hands, pleading to the tow truck driver,

Drama Dolls

the pulled hair on his head remained sticking up in the air.

Reaching the scene, Lena gave the baseball back to Jeffrey.

Explaining the situation, the tow truck driver said, "I'm just doing my job."

"But I'm right here," Jeffrey said. His hands up, palms facing the sun, Jeffrey's elbows were at right angles. Demanding the tow truck driver release his car, he said, "Don't you have better things to do?"

Staying professional, not letting his curiosity get the best of him, the operator, standing erect in front of Jeffrey, said, "I'll release your car for two hundred dollars."

Lena's mouth dropped. The sticker shock caused her body to collapse.

The voice inside, it was cursing the tow truck driver out.

Erupting out of his skin, Jeffrey said, "That's ridiculous!"

Red lips on his face, unable to keep composure, the man said, "You know what's ridiculous? You showing up like Ronald fucking McDonald."

Offended, her body straightening, Lena jumped to Jeffrey's side. She said, "I think he looks nice."

Cocking his head toward the pretty Doll, he said, "And who are you, Mrs. McDonald?"

Getting in between the man and Lena, Jeffrey raised his finger to the operator's face. "You leave her out of this."

"I'll leave you both out of this if you pay me two hundred dollars," the man said. Eying the baseball in Jeffrey's hand, he said, "*And* that baseball."

Stiffening his body, the anger inside brooding, his teeth starting to show as his eyes grew to the size of softballs, Jeffrey said, "What?! I caught this ball fair and square!"

Stomping his feet, hard into the pavement, he screamed, "You can't take my ball!" Parading around in a circle before them, Jeffrey continued to stomp.

His face collapsing, wrinkles appearing from all angles, Jeffrey started to cry. "He wants to take my ball!" Screaming at the top of his lungs, stomping louder, he said, "My ball!"

Jeffrey folded his arms, close to his chest, protecting his coveted souvenir. Glaring at the man, eyes wet from tears, he said, "I won't let you take my ball!"

The change in behavior forced the tow truck driver to step back.

Lena, seeing Jeffrey slipping into a dark place, said, "It's OK." Rubbing Jeffrey on the shoulder, she whispered, "I'll take care of this."

Drama Dolls

Holding his breath, his face turning as red as his lips, Jeffrey's body started to tremble.

Whispering to Jeffrey, Lena said, "Just calm down." She placed her hands on his shoulders. Jeffrey's body, it was still shaking. "I'll take care of this." Looking deeply into Jeffrey's eyes, she said, "Don't worry."

Holding up her finger to the man, Lena walked Jeffrey away from the scene. Coming up to a parking bumper, Lena pointed down at the concrete parking stop. "Can you sit right here?" she said.

Caressing the baseball, hugging it close to him, Jeffrey complied and sat. Leaning into the ball, he whispered, "I won't let them take you away too." Jeffrey kissed the ball and then cradled it.

The tow driver leaned in forward to observe the crying Drama Doll. His mouth fallen open, he stared in curiosity at the tearful Jeffrey.

Returning to the truck operator, Lena pleaded with him. "Listen. If you let him keep the ball, I'll pay you two-fifty for the car." Looking back at Jeffrey, she said, "He just lost his wife."

Peeking over Lena, the driver's expression softening, he said, "I'll tell you what. Just take care of him. I'll give the car back. No charge."

Lena's body sank in relief. Displaying an endearing

141

look toward the man, Lena smiled. "Thank you," she said. She extended her frame, standing up on tip toes, and kissed his cheek. "Thank you," she said again.

The man put his hands up in surrender. Taking one last look at the vulnerable cheerleader, he said, "Seriously. Take care of him." He cringed and then jumped into his truck.

The tow truck receding into the distance, Lena plopped down next to Jeffrey and put her arm around his waist. Swaying left to right, a calming motion as if she was trying to put a baby asleep, Lena finally turned to Jeffrey.

Cradling the ball close, his eyes red from crying, Jeffrey smiled at the ball.

Sitting on the parking stoop was an eternity. Stretching her legs out in front of her, Lena leaned her body back and looked up to the clear sky. There was not a cloud around, only a straight shot to Heaven. Both her spouse and Jeffrey's looking down at them. Lena, she wondered if the two had met. If they, also, had bereavement groups for losing someone. Was Heaven one big baseball game to attend? These thoughts and more passed through her mind.

A soothing breeze picked up, blowing her hair into her face. Opening her eyes, her vision focusing on the pale blue backdrop in between strands of hair, Lena

Drama Dolls

exhaled softly out of her nose.

Staring into the ground in front of her, she said, "Are you OK?"

Nodding his head, Jeffrey said, "Yeah." His voice, it was innocent and soft. The ball was warm and sticky from the heat. The smell of leather in his nose, he said, "We can go."

He looked around to see that the tow truck driver was gone. "Where's—"

"I took care of it," Lena said.

The pair stood and entered the Corvette. Starting the car, the radio's volume turned up, Jeffrey shifted into drive.

A circle of light led Barb and Brittney up the staircase toward the bedrooms. Leading the heist, gripping the flashlight with one hand, Barb took each step with caution. Brittney followed behind. Pillowcases slung around their shoulders, the dynamic duo stopped on the landing that joined the bedrooms of the house.

Mask situated, cheerleader uniform freshly washed, Brittney struck a pose. Her fist on one hip while her other arm extended into the air. Legs straight and flexed, the Drama Doll's skirt was just above her bare knees.

Her lower legs shaved and smooth, her ankle socks the same length, Brittney muffled the words, "Ready? OK!" This time around Brittney's wig hair was tied back into a pony tail.

The mask pulled down tight over Brittney's chin, Barb could tell that she had pride in her appearance.

Sighing, reluctant to participate, Barb gave Brittney a look.

Brittney didn't budge. Her body still stiff in posture. Flexing her limbs, Brittney's legs began to shake.

Staring at the cheerleader as her body trembled with each second that passed, Barb rolled her eyes. Giving in, mirroring the pose, opposite hand on her hip, free hand lifting up her mask, Barb said, "OK." Pulling down the mask over her face, she extended her hand into the air.

Brittney, pumping her open fist, she cheered, "Dee, ar, ay, em, ay, what're we gonna do today? We're gonna rob, we're gonna thieve, we're take this shit then leave; We're gonna run, we're gonna hide, we're gonna sort this shit inside; My house, my house, as quiet as a mouse."

Barb stared as Brittney announced the anthem.

"Dee, oh, el, el, es, we'll be out in thirty or less; We're gonna dress, as our best, we're gonna wear high skirts and breasts; We're gonna cheer, we're gonna play, Drama Dolls are here to stay!"

Drama Dolls

Standing like a statue, waiting for the conclusion, Barb dropped her head to her chest.

Finishing the cheer, Brittney said, "Drama Dolls!"

The cheerleaders broke position, and then went to work. Inside the master, the flashlight stationed on the drawer to give them light, the masculine cheerleaders assessed the situation. The Victorian homes' ceilings were tall to give them open space. Having gone through the house with the realtor reduced the time to get in and out.

Walking toward a closet, Brittney said, "You take the drawers." A hollow expression from Barb, Brittney opened a walk-in and stepped inside. In a row on the shelf above the clothing rods were designer shoes, boots, and sandals. Women's shoes galore. Jimmy Choo, Sam Edelman, TOMS Wedge Booties, Vince Camuto, and Dolce Vita. The boots were by Munro and Paul Green.

Pulling down shoes into her case, the bag began to fill up quickly. Once the shelf was clear, Brittney looked down at the clothing rod.

Gowns from Aidan Mattox and Adam Lippes were hung by color. Lined up like they had been placed in a particular order, Brittney stepped back to admire the clothing. Jaw dropping, her lips curled into a smile.

In the mix were sleeveless crewneck crepe gowns, beaded bodice full-skirt gowns, and half-sleeve gowns with

145

bow shoulders. Squeezing them together with her hands, Brittney pulled them down from the rack and threw them out onto the floor.

Empty shoe boxes lined the wall. She kicked them over to make sure nothing was inside. Tumbling over, the cardboard boxes fell onto each other, making a Stonehenge-like stack in the corner.

Startled by the falling boxes, cutting Brittney a look, Barb said, "What was that?"

Stepping out, Brittney was shaking her head. She said, "Nothing." Turning the flashlight so it pointed to the vanity, she grabbed an empty pillowcase and began pulling out drawers.

Before Brittney's eyes was a huge collection of cosmetics. Some used and others never having been opened. Foundation bottles, brand new, the caps tightly sealed, were thrown into the bag.

Eyeliner, blush, lipstick, the score provoked Brittney into stealing makeup for herself.

Mascara, eye shadow, fingernail polish, they were all taken from their drawer slots. Pulling out each item, reading the label as she went, Brittney tossed the individual pieces into her bag.

Closing each drawer, returning it to position, the cheerleader stepped back and looked at the vanity. During

Drama Dolls

the tour, the group had not been allowed to enter the master, so admiring the piece of furniture was a first. "Beautiful," she said.

The hand-carved cabriolet legs on the dressing table were classy. The smooth curves made for a great piece. In the beveled mirror, Barb's reflection poured through dresser drawers. Separating T-shirts and socks, Barb felt her hand along the drawer's inside and up and down the corners.

"What're you doing?" Brittney said to the mirrored image.

Through the glass, Barb's reflection turned toward Brittney. Her cardboard breasts uneven underneath the sweater, she said, "Sometimes people stash valuables in the back of dressers." Never having had to justify her actions before, Barb said, "Why?"

"Oh." Brittney answered with a shrug. She said, "Just asking."

Instead of continuing on the vanity, Brittney watched Barb move to each drawer. The way she moved, it was as if she was gliding on air. Barb had studied the movement of gymnasts and ballet dancers so that she could incorporate the graceful motion into her secret identity. Sliding on the wood floor, elegantly rearranging the articles of clothing, Barb stylishly maneuvered through the fabric.

The next drawer, filled with shorts and yoga pants, also came up empty. Closing the drawer shut, Barb pulled at the next bin. The wood sticking together, expanded from the humidity, the Drama Doll yanked it out. The frustration caused the wooden drawer to fall down to the floor.

Articles of clothing went everywhere. Spread out around Barb as she moved away from the fallen drawer.

Scattered amongst the sweatpants and workout clothes was a gun. A black semiautomatic. Single stack. A holy-fuck-you-just-found-a-gun!

Stepping back, the nosy Doll craned her neck toward Brittney. Returning to the weapon, Barb kneeled to collect the piece. She held up the gun in plain view, spinning it around slowly to examine it.

Brittney's eyes bulged underneath her mask. The scene unfolding through the mirror's reflection.

The voice of scared shitless reason said, "Oh my God, oh my God! She's got a gun. She's got a gun!"

Brittney dropped her pillowcase. The makeup containers crashed, some opening. The foundation glass bottles were loud on the hardwood. One bottle cracked, causing it to spill inside the bag. A peach colored spot formed on the pillowcase.

Drama Dolls

Through the mirrored image, Barb was inspecting the firearm closely. Twisting it around, she observed the hammer, magazine, and the grip. Groping the piece, Barb felt the slide and barrel under her fingertips. She pointed it at Brittney, her arm extended out. A flick of her wrist, the gun going up toward the ceiling, acting as if she was pulling the trigger.

In the mirror, the muzzle pointed at Brittney's back. Raising her hands in slow motion, Brittney played the part of victim. The reverse-imaged Barb released her position.

Turning around, Brittney walked toward her counterpart. Together, the two stared at the semiautomatic, their phony smiles close to the gun. Brittney leaned in closer until the thermoplastic polymer was touching. Pulling back, Brittney removed the mask, her mouth dropping open.

Heart beating faster, Brittney said, "Is it loaded?"

Headlights came in through the window. The man cheerleaders ducked, the gun still between them. Barb shrugged. She said, "Should we take it?"

The headlights rolled across the walls and then disappeared. Almost pitch black in the room, the only illumination came from the flashlight pointing toward the vanity. The mirror revealed the shine and blinded Brittney for a moment.

"I don't think so." Her eyes went wide. Eyebrows up, Brittney said, "Put it back."

Barb, she was frozen without movement.

Stepping backward to add separation, Brittney, she said, "Seriously, put it back."

Barb nodded, her mask displaying a ghostly smile. "OK," she said. Her voice, calm and non-threatening, she said, "I'll put it back." Her white gloved finger was holding the gun by its trigger guard. The semiautomatic swinging, its barrel swaying back and forth. Fingering the guard, Barb placed it into the drawer and put it back into the dresser.

The cheerleaders made eye contact. Barb through her mask and Brittney for real. They nodded, a mutual agreement, and then continued with the lift.

A hairbrush with clumped hair strands was stashed in a small nightstand beside the bed. Inhaling the brush's scent, its aroma, reminded Brittney of Her. The smell of shampoo, Her scalp, emanating from the bristles. The similar scent, possibly the same shampoo and conditioner, made Brittney emotional. Her knees buckled, causing her to fall downward temporarily. Straightening her legs, Brittney stood like a statue, breathing in the smell under her nose.

Drama Dolls

The excitement from the ball game, the heist, it evaporated into depression. Brittney's stomach began to convulse, a dry heave of crying pouring out of her. Pulling the brush into her, she rubbed her nostrils over the bristles. The brush tickled her nose. Scratching her nose with her finger, her eyes red and burning, Brittney wiped her eyes repeatedly. Standing in the dark, she closed her eyes tight.

Barb continued to pile the bags with goods, ignoring the scene in front of her. Grabbing items with her hand, whatever could fit in her palm, she threw down into the pillowcase.

A long humming escaped Brittney's slightly opened mouth. A tear building, falling down her face. Shaking her head vigorously until the feelings went away, opening her eyes, Brittney exhaled. Mask falling from her hand, the fragrance from the brush causing her to drop it.

Barb moved from her position, stepping over articles of clothing, makeup containers, and a small garbage can. Looking down into the trash as she passed over it, something jumped out at her.

Reaching down inside the garbage, Barb found an unused tampon. The wrapper stuck to the inside of the trash can's bag. She picked it out, its cloudy white surface fresh out of the packaging. There was a lipstick-drawn circle in the center. To mimic a period.

Barb looked over at Brittney as she breathed in the hair. Brittney's mask still on the floor by her feet. Holding the tampon between her fingers, watching what Brittney had become, Barb stuffed the tampon down into her garter.

Coming out of her pity party, regaining composure, Brittney walked past Barb and moved to the next bedroom.

Another guest bedroom, used as a dumping ground, was bare. An area rug plopped down in the middle, positioned equidistant from each wall, was storage for moving boxes.

Rows of boxes with their flaps up, you could see the entire guts with one swoop. The contents were scattered in unorganized piles. The boxes filled to the top with mismatched jewels.

Sorting through the mess, searching for the valuable pieces of jewelry, Brittney picked out a couple different items. A diamond solitaire pendant in 18k white gold, a 14k gold double heart diamond pendant, a bracelet with a circular yellow gold photo locket, and a confetti drop necklace with diamonds.

Princess cut diamond solitaire studs, wisteria pearl earrings, white Kyocera opal earrings shaped like

Drama Dolls

teardrops, the gems were all collected in one scoop. Kneeling on the carpet before the boxes, Brittney took her time digging through the valuables.

The voice of immature reason said, "It's like a real life claw game."

One box contained various types of trinkets. Chain bib necklaces, gold color hoop earrings, metal hinged bracelets, and polished bangle bracelets in sterling silver.

Necklaces knotted together were left behind. Earrings without pairs or backs, they were tossed aside. Cupping items in her hand, Barb's footsteps moving down the hall behind her, Brittney got to her feet and examined the rest of the room.

The only other thing in the room was a moveable coat rack. Suits hanging from the rack's rod, the pants folded over the hangers with their respective coats draped over, were color coordinated from light to dark.

"All the clothes in this house," the voice of curious reason said.

Flipping through the selection, the suit sizes looked familiar. Brittney collected them all and stashed them into the pillowcase. Folding them in half and then pushing them into the bags, Brittney left the rack empty.

Barb screamed from downstairs, "Let's roll!"

Running flat footed down the street, the weight of the bags were hard on her knees. With her skirt flailing from the motion, Brittney slowed to a jog.

Barb followed suit. The cheerleaders, they decreased their speed to a walk. The night was hot and sticky like the rest of them. High summer temperatures started to take their toll on the path to freedom. Holding the bags became harder and having their heads covered in plastic was a challenge.

Barb's face was wet from trapped sweat underneath her mask. Lifting up her mask above her mouth so she could feel the air, Barb took a quick glance toward Brittney.

Plodding forward, steady in her pace, Brittney kept to herself.

Far enough away, pushing through the wooded escape trail, Barb moved the bags from shoulder to shoulder. Her pom-poms were lost in the stream. Her white shoes, they were peppered with brown mud spots. And her ankle socks were stained with dirty water.

Broaching the subject, Barb said, "What did you find in that room?" She was breathing heavy from the getaway and periodically would raise her mask to get some air on her face.

Drama Dolls

Taking short breaths, breathing hard out of her mouth, Brittney said, "Just some boxes filled with jewelry. All kinds." Stepping over a branch, she said, "There were a shitload of diamond necklaces. Stuff like that."

Showing concern for her friend, Barb said, "You feeling alright?"

"What do you mean?"

Walking ahead on the single lane trail, Barb said, "You broke down back there."

"I'm fine." The leaves breaking under her feet, Brittney watched a rabbit running alongside. The hopping sounded like a potato chip bag being twisted. The rabbit stopped, burying its face into a pile of leaves. When it pulled up to run away, the pile of leaves uncovered something shiny.

Brittney walked faster toward the object, the distance between her and Barb increasing.

Following behind, picking up her pace, Barb said, "What?"

Bending down, collecting the medium gauge curb chained piece, Brittney rose to her feet and held it up.

Her gait now a trot, edging up next to Brittney, Barb said, "Is that a necklace?"

Ducking into the alley, squatting behind the area

where the dumpsters met the buildings, a smell of french fries touched Brittney's nose. With nothing in her stomach all day save for the cup of coffee at the diner and the beer at the stadium, she was feeling woozy.

The foundation on her skin began to itch. The blush more like blobs than circles. Brittney could taste the lipstick on her tongue. The inside of the mask, its plastic was now a smeared maroon.

Breathing in the salty potatoes, the stench entering the tiny hole on the mask's nose, her insides began to growl. Trapped underneath the plastic, the lingering fries surrounded her. Brittney pushed the dumpster away from her to gain some separation.

"You OK?" Barb said.

Nodding, breathing in the mix of Chinese food and mayonnaise-covered fries, Brittney closed her eyes. Her heart was racing. Her breathing heavy.

Her knees buckling from hunger, Brittney collapsed down onto the asphalt.

Dropping the pillowcases on the gravel, the tops came undone. The uneven streets caused pieces to fall out. Bracelets rolling into sewers, earrings into cracked pavement. Handfuls of jewelry spilling out onto the pavement.

Barb ran over to Brittney. Heaving her up,

Drama Dolls

propping her against the building, Barb said, "Brittney!" Shaking her with no luck, she said, "Brittney!"

There were sounds of water drops below in the sewer. Plopping down the drain were bracelets and miscellaneous items.

Screaming at the top of her lungs, Barb said, "Brittney!"

Brittney's head collapsed on her chest, causing her to slide down the side of the building.

Barb flexed her thighs, pushing the Doll back up straight. "Brittney!" When there was no response, Barb said, "Jeffrey!" Using her elbow to keep the distressed Drama Doll standing, Barb slapped her across the face. Stepping in closer, Barb said, "Jeffrey!"

Opening her eyes, through the little holes, Brittney could see Barb's face was very close. There was a sham smile in view. Barb's artificial eyes were open wide. The recovering cheerleader could see the thermosoftening plastic stretched out. The tear strength and heat resistant face was a quality product.

Waving her hand in front of the lightheaded Drama Doll, Barb said, "You alright, Jeffrey?"

In and out of focus, shaking her head, the mask rearranged itself around Brittney's face. She said, "You never call me Jeffrey."

157

Under their feet, narrow cuff bracelets, triple-wrap leather, and waxed cord bracelets rolled down the acute slope, some down the street, and others into cracks. More bracelets, thick bangle bracelets, into the sewer.

Pushing Barb away from her, running toward the drain, Brittney said, "Nooooo!"

Behind her, Barb, she said, "It's OK. It's OK."

Turning around, Brittney screamed in panic. Her hands grabbing at jewels as they rolled past. In desperation, she said, "Don't just stand there! Help!"

Running to her side, Barb kneeled to retrieve the valuables. The both of them on hands and knees. In full costume getup, they were searching the alley for lost jewels.

Brittney was frantic. She was also hungry. Her body starting to shake from not eating.

The Drama Dolls threw earrings into the bags as they found them. Tossing various bracelets on top of the earrings.

The voice of worried reason, it was screaming at Brittney to keep looking.

Ripping off her mask so she could see better, Brittney continued the search. Collecting the jewelry, returning them to the pillowcases, Brittney started to calm down.

Drama Dolls

Rolling through the dark alley, the car's headlights off, the engine's purr was a stray cat. Lena flashed her lights. Leaning closer to the windshield, looking out into the alley, Lena said, "What the...?"

Brittney and Barb's silhouettes were like animals grazing. Eyes half closed from the sudden flash, Brittney motioned for Lena to come out.

Sliding out of the getaway car, Lena said, "What's going on?"

Her face in disarray, Brittney said, "Don't talk. Just help."

Open pillowcases surrounding them, the contents were wet and filled with gravel. The three cheerleaders ensuring each piece returned to the bags.

Pain in her gut, stomach growling, Brittney crawled over to the drain and looked down into the water. Her knees were scraped from the sharp rocks on the pavement. Dirt on her gloves, Brittney's uniform was getting brown from the filth. Pressing her face into the sewer cover, the rust and mud stained Brittney's cosmetics-riddled face. Orange and black splattered across her smile. Her hair began clumping together from the debris.

Barb looked at Lena. She shook her head and then turned and began tossing the bags into the backseat. Filled from previous heists, Barb had trouble closing the door. Pushing the pillowcases into each other, the opposite door opened.

Falling out of the car, her body half out, Emily's mask fell off her head and onto the pebbles.

"Emily!" Brittney said, standing from her crouch. Running toward her, she stopped suddenly. Turning to Lena, she said, "Where's my mask?"

The car was running, the alley smelling like a buffet, and Lena was scanning the pavement for Brittney's mask. Spotting it near the foot of a dumpster, she reached down, wiped off the debris, and picked it up.

"Here you go," Lena said, handing it over to Brittney.

Brittney, replacing her expression so the passed out Doll would not see her that way, retrieved Emily's mask. It was dirty from the fall. Brittney brushed the plastic appearance on her leg. Rubbing the mask hard, slapping it across her knee, Brittney scraped some filth off the mask's forehead.

Barb was pulling Emily back into the car when Lena appeared behind Brittney.

Putting her hand on Brittney's shoulder, Lena said, "We've got to go." Tapping her softly, attempting to calm the cheerleader down, Lena said, "Now."

Drama Dolls

Ignoring her counterpart, Brittney continued to wipe down the plastic. When the disguise was free of rubbish, she leaned into the window and replaced the mask, straightening it until she looked beautiful again.

Stomach growling, a pain deep in her gut, Brittney said, "I need to eat."

The mask's thick plastic material stifled the words as they rang through the speaker. The food order was faint and inaudible.

Exiting the speaker system, cracking into the air, the voice said, "Free what?" The employee working the night shift said, "I can't understand you, ma'am."

The car's engine at a hum, positioned on the drive-thru censor, Lena shifted into park. Speaking louder and enunciating each word, she said, "I'll take three number sevens!"

Out the speaker, the voice, repeating what it had heard, said, "Free never heaven? I don't know what you're saying, miss." Annoyed, the voice said, "Please speak clearly into the speaker."

The food menu was bright in the darkness of the night. The value meal options were surrounding the speaker, each item numbered for easy ordering. The glow of the large sign shined through the distance.

Littering the spaces of the near empty parking lot was a trickle of cars.

Lifting up the mask above her mouth, Lena shouted into the speaker holes, "Three number sevens."

Emily, falling down in her seat, her head leaned back on the headrest. Her arms were flailed out across her from the drive. Her knees spread eagle in front of her. Next to her, on the floor mat between her shoes, were bags piled on top of each other.

"What do you want to drink with the meals?"

Lena, pinching the bottom part of her mask, curling it up over her lips, said, "Three Cokes."

"Anything else?" the voice in the speaker said.

"That's all." Lena pulled the phony expression down over her chin.

The voice, loud and echoing, said, "Please pull forward."

The neon lights under the fast food restaurant's roof illuminated the car's interior. A trio of glowing bodies sitting upright with one shadowed from herself. Bags of jewelry cramped together throughout the back seat and the floor mats. The car was packed tight like a can of sardines.

In front of the Buick, a group of young men exited a parked sedan and then entered into the restaurant.

Rolling up to the window, the cheerleaders

Drama Dolls

stopped in front of the glass box of the restaurant.

The teenager working the shift stuck her head out to greet the ghostly crew. Lena's mask was in the window. She had a smile with perfect teeth. Her lips were a nude rose color. Big blue eyes, Lena's eyelashes were fanned out evenly across her forehead. She had circles for cheeks. Pin holes for nostrils. And her hair was combed down the sides of her face.

Startled, the window employee whispered /screamed, "Jesus!" Her heart skipping a beat, she placed her palm on her chest. Her mouth falling open, she had no idea what to think. Staring into the car window, the ghostly mask silent, the window worker burst into laughter. "Jesus Christ!" she said in between chortles. Her body frozen, the employee's laughter gave way to silence.

Hearing the commotion, Brittney leaned forward and looked over Lena's shoulder. Now there were two ghostly mugs in the drive-thru worker's face. Two very happy, smiling doll faces wearing cheerleader outfits, ordering fast food in the middle of the night.

"What the hell?" The window worker, once humored, was now ecstatic and frightened at the same time.

The back window slowly rolled down. The employee's reflection disappeared off the glass as the window bowled downward. There was another hollow expression in her sight. Turning back to address the driver, holding in a smile, she said, "That'll be nineteen forty." Swallowing hard, the employee's eyes widened.

Behind her, a co-worker appeared, holding a drink holder. There were three cups filled with soda. Peeking around the employee, the co-worker started laughing. The drink cups were shaking from the laughter. Almost dropping the cups out the drive-thru window, the colleague balanced the holder, straightening the drinks.

Lena passed a twenty through the drive-up window. Her white gloved fingers pinching the bill. Her bare arm uncovered, the color of her skin a smidgen darker than the artificial skin on her mask.

The employee, she said, "Tyrese, come look at this." One by one, employee after employee, crowding into the small area, they all came to look at the freak show in the LeSabre.

Heads peering around each other, the scene bled into the dining room of the joint. Customers stopping in after bar hopping, they all craned their heads, in between ordering, to witness the clown car. Stepping up on their toes to get a better look. Pointing, joining in on the excitement, one patron whipped out a cell phone to capture a photo.

Drama Dolls

"Oh my God!" Tyrese said. He pointed past Barb. "There's one sleeping." Jumping up and down in excitement, he said, "Look at her!"

As the food and drinks were being passed through the window, the fast food workers snapped their own pictures with cell phones. Unfazed, the Drama Dolls continued with their business as if nothing unusual was occurring.

An employee, poking her head out to get a better look, said, "Thank you. Have a nice night." Pulling in, she burst out laughing.

Lena pulled out into the parking lot and stopped the car. Handing the burgers out to each cheerleader, fries soon after, the trio removed their masks and ate.

Brittney, she stared into the bright yellow lights around the building throwing down a handful of french fries. The salt was burning her lips. The taste of potato paper on her tongue.

The voice of hungry reasoning, it said, "I'm lovin' this."

Stomach past the point of hunger, the feeling like something was squeezing her kidney, Brittney downed her food without ever enjoying a taste. Past the brink of tiredness, Brittney Doll just stared into the glittery lights of the restaurant.

Lena, biting down into the burger, looked at Barb through the rearview.

And Barb, she slowly eyed Brittney and then Emily. Then back again. Eating her burger with force, swallowing hard, Barb shook her head in revulsion. One fry at a time was popped into her mouth, as the three cheerleaders sat eating without a sound.

Rolling into the garage, the car's tires came to a screech. Lena shifted into park and then opened her door. The beeping of the getaway car door echoed in the stall as the garage door closed.

The lingering smell of fast food filtered out into the bay. Brittney stepped out and moved around to the backseat.

Grabbing the bags, one at a time, the Dolls threw them into the house until they were finished. Before Brittney could say a word, Barb said, "I know, let her sleep." She slammed the door behind her.

Emily, through the window, was slouched down against the door. Her head leaned back into the headrest. Shoes on backward, they were tied in knots. Her sweater was tucked into her skirt. Although the crop of hair was uncombed over her face, Emily was still beautiful.

Barb and Lena took their positions in the living

Drama Dolls

room, leaving Brittney behind.

There were two big piles of stash, one called the soaking wet jewels and the other called gems to go through later. The bags of wet gems, soaked and muddy, sat in the corner of the room, away from them. There was a smell of muddy fabric hanging in the air above. The bags became crustier each second, drying to a crunchy material.

The living room was sticky. Without a central air system, Brittney had resorted to putting air conditioning units in windows throughout the house. The stretch of hot days caused the room to feel humid. The dirty water from the soaked jewelry smelled stronger than usual.

Barb pinched her sweater, pulling it away from her chest. Back and forth, in a quick fashion, the Drama Doll attempted to cool herself.

Lena, alternatively, wiped the sweat from her bare arms.

Pulling Emily into the house, Brittney brought the passed out cheerleader up the long flight of stairs. The punch drunk Doll's legs dragging across the area rugs and hardwood in the process. Again, the emotional cheerleader made excuses for her being passed out. "She's sick with the flu." And, "I don't want to leave her alone while in this condition."

The excuses, they were second nature to Brittney.

167

Exiting her mouth like verbal diarrhea. "It's been a long day."

Collecting tiny pockets of cool air with every pull of her shirt, Barb did not offer up a response for the excuse. Instead, she just rolled her eyes.

Lena, though, played along. She said, "I understand. The flu could take you out for days." Talking up the staircase, watching Brittney disappear with the useless cheerleader, Lena's vision returned to Barb.

Barb was staring at Lena with a dumbfounded look. Lena's smile suddenly vanished. Looking at each other, surrounded by a pile of wet gems and muddy bags, Lena said, "What?"

When Brittney was completely out of sight, Barb pulled out the tampon from her garter belt.

Lena laughed. She said, "A beautiful cheerleader playing her part?"

Flashing it in front of her, Barb's eyes grew bigger. Her neck pushing forward, urging her on.

"What?" Lena said. She bellowed a high phony laugh. "You're getting into character. That's hilarious!" Up above them, the two could hear footsteps moving from one side of the room to the other.

Shaking her head, pointing to the drawn in circle on the tampon, Barb whispered, "This was in the

Drama Dolls

garbage." A loud crash overhead startled Barb. She looked up, her head ducking automatically.

Lena shrugged, her hands palms up in the air. "So," she said.

Whispering each word carefully, Barb said, "This. Was. In. The. Garbage." Up above, more footsteps circled the bed. The noise stopped for a moment, and then picked back up. Looking up to the ceiling, Barb could hear the steps moving toward the staircase.

Lena, cocking her head toward the ceiling, displayed a gesture as if a lightbulb turned on in her head. She mouthed, "Oh!" and then the two became silent.

Before another word could be uttered, hearing the faint talking from the staircase, Brittney emerged from the second floor.

Acting as if everything was normal, Lena said, "Welcome back."

Barb, cupping the tampon in her hand against her wrist, smiled.

Brittney sat down and the three began to sort.

The stacks of random items shrank to a bearable few designated piles of necklaces, bracelets, rings, and tiaras. Lena placed a shiny tiara on her head. She was a queen posing, her arm in an angle with her hand flat, flicking back and forth. Her palm alternating with the top of her hand.

Barb, placing the final tiara in its place, said, "All hail the queen."

Still cupping the tampon against her wrist, Barb slowly slid it behind her back away from view. "What do you want to do, Brittney?" she said.

Brittney, painfully full and half-awake, said, "Let's build a pyramid." Her emotions running the full gamut, Brittney had experienced the five stages of grief all at once.

The discovery of the gun had altered their routine while in the house. More times than not, Barb and Brittney would celebrate during the burglary. The feeling of getting away with something was liberating. Jumping on the bed, rolling around into the blankets like sardines, or building a fort with pillows were but a few of the joys they had partaken in.

Now, though, the scene was getting weird.

"Let's what?" Barb said, the words coming out stifled. Dropping the tampon down the back of her skirt, holding it close with the skirt's garter, she said, "A pyramid?" Surveying the room, amidst the stack of jewels and the existing furniture, Barb said, "Here?"

Lena, her body erect, she stood in a tree position. One leg bent outward, her foot on her inner thigh, her right arm straight into the air and her left arm, bent opposite her leg with her fist into her hip. "Brittney said, 'Let's build a pyramid,'" she echoed.

Barb was cautious. She stood watching the two Drama Dolls make room for the three cheerleader pyramid. Without lending a hand, Barb's body stiff and aloof, Lena gently nudged her to participate. They had a brief stare down, and before Barb could speak, Lena showed her clenched teeth.

Barb, mouthing the word, "Tampon," shook her head.

Her neck jutting forward, the whites of her teeth in sight, eyes enlarging, Lena's silent rage scared Barb into her body.

Barb fell back, reserved for a moment, and then finally gave in.

"C'mon," Brittney said. "It'll be fun!" Making room for the trio, Brittney rearranged the end tables. She pushed small stacks of valuables away from them. Scanning the area rug for loose pieces, she said, "You already dogged me out with the baseball game."

Interjecting, Lena said, "Which was fun by the way."

Building the base of one corner, kneeling on the floor with her hands flat in front of her, Brittney looked at Barb to follow suit.

Begrudgingly, Barb caved in and dropped down to the floor. There was a long cylindrical bulge coming from the back of her skirt. Side by side, their bodies in yoga cow positions, Lena propped herself up to make the top.

Feeling Lena's knees in the small of her back, Brittney arched her body to accommodate the weight. The sharp kneecaps digging into her, Brittney adjusted her position. She slowly straightened out so Lena could balance properly. Sucking in her abs, her posture stiffened. The positioning caused Brittney's arms to shake as if she was holding on to an electric fence.

Flexing her triceps, steadying her arms, Brittney nudged Barb with her elbow. Staring into the sofa, she said, "You lead."

In her own tabletop position, Barb rolled her eyes. She said, "Ready?"

Lena and Brittney, they simultaneously said, "OK."

On both knees, her upper torso lengthening, Lena slow clapped a steady rhythm. "Give me a dee. Give me an ar. Give me an ay. Give me an em. Give me another ay." Her clapping becoming louder and louder, bouncing off the walls, she said, "What's that spell?"

Looking straight, body stern, Brittney said, "Drama!"

Drama Dolls

"What's that spell?"

"Drama!"

And Barb, next to Brittney, her body limp and uninterested, she whispered, "Drama," without energy.

"Say it again," Lena said. "Drama!" Shooting her right fist into the air, her balance adjusted, causing her to crash down to the floor.

Feeling Lena next to her, Brittney turned to catch her, with Lena only falling the remaining distance with Brittney's arms around her waist.

Lena laughed, her body shaking in excitement.

"Are you alright?" Brittney said.

Laughing, her face turning red, a smile covering half of it, Lena said, "That was so fun!"

Annoyed, unwilling to go on, Barb stood to her feet. She said, "Let's just see what we got." Barb quickly collected the random stacks that were pushed aside. When the remaining cheerleaders were out of the way, Barb returned the end tables to their positions.

Getting back to business, sorting through the heists' contents, Barb sat focused on the job in front of her. Silently fuming, grabbing each necklace one by one and placing them into separate stacks, Barb began to breathe heavier. Her exhaling visible. A din of air erupting out of her nostrils.

The voice of obvious reason, it said, "Somebody's pissed off."

Concerned, breaking up the tension, Lena said, "How's Emily?" Her voice was soft. Quiet.

"She is," Brittney said, each word separated by a pause, "resting."

Barb's eyes moved toward Brittney. Her hand picking and sorting without stopping. Throwing the jewelry into their respective piles, she shook her head in disgust. The air becoming thick between them, silence now eerie, Barb stopped all motion. A few items still in her grasp.

Abrupt and to the point, throwing a bracelet hard into the floor while her other palm fisted around another, Barb said, "We can't keep taking her."

Lena froze. Her body rising from its position, moving back to evacuate the area without drawing attention to herself. Her eyes moving sideways, she slid back into her seat to gain distance from the two.

Brittney's mood switched. Building to a fume, she yelled, "Get out!" Pointing to the front door, she said, "Get the fuck out!"

Holding a bangle bracelet in her hand, staring into Brittney's eyes, Barb opened her mouth. She wanted to say something but instead just stood up.

Drama Dolls

Dropping the accessory, walking toward the entry way, Barb turned and said, "We're better off without her." Turning the handle and opening the door, she said, "*You're better off. Trust me.*"

Lena hesitated. Caught in the middle, deciding to stay neutral for the time being, she slowly followed. She had no other choice. "I'll call you later," she said to Brittney.

Brittney, her glare zoning in on Barb, did not utter a word.

Lena, leaning into Brittney's sightline, said, "OK?"

Halfway down the staircase, Barb disappeared from the scene.

A breeze of sticky air entered the house, brushing up against Lena as she stood stationary in the doorway.

In the living room, the irate Doll's eyes were locked on the spot where they last saw Barb, looking past the statue-still Lena and into the darkness.

Closing the door behind her, Lena paused and then poked her head inside the house. She whispered, "I'll call you," and then disappeared from the Victorian.

Alone in the room, the heat becoming unbearable, Brittney walked up the staircase. Taking hard steps, stomping up the wood flight, she walked toward her bedroom. Passing the answering machine, the blinking red light showing new messages, Brittney entered her bedroom and closed the door behind her.

Stripping out of the cheerleader outfit, her face still splattered with makeup, Brittney/Jeffrey slid into bed with Emily.

Emily was naked underneath the covers, undressed by Jeffrey when he brought her upstairs. Sleeping, passed out, dead, whatever tripped Jeffrey's trigger, Emily did exactly what he wanted her to do. A RealDoll consisting of a poseable skeleton and silicone flesh, Emily had been purchased after She died.

Unable to let go, and not wanting to be alone, Jeffrey had ordered the life-sized flexible mannequin when an Internet advertisement popped up on his browser while visiting an adult website.

Designed to be as realistic as a human female, Jeffrey had maxed out his credit card with the anticipation that he could temporarily replace his wife until he finished grieving.

Dressing up Emily was difficult at first. Jeffrey had never dressed anyone but himself, so sliding on panties and pulling shirts over her upper body was new to him. Ordering a doll with the same measurements as his wife, he was able to save money by reusing Her clothes.

176

Drama Dolls

Working it out with his inner voice, Jeffrey insisted that Emily was not taking the place of Her. Merely wearing Her clothes was a way for Jeffrey to remember Her and save money at the same time.

The voice of "killing two birds with one stone" reason said, "I love how your brain works."

The sturdiness of the RealDoll was worth the money. Platinum silicone was stronger so the doll would not tear, so the longevity would last as long as Jeffrey needed it to.

He turned to Emily. Still distraught from the encounter with William, Jeffrey said, "He can't tell me what to do." She remained lifeless as he stroked her hair. Jeffrey pulled her in close to him.

"OK?" Jeffrey said to her. Emily was unresponsive. She had the same expression as before. Her eyes seducing you when you look at her. Her lips, full, and ready for action. Blackish straight hair that was interchangeable with a blonde wig with a trace of sandy brown.

Emily's sultry eyes were olive colored. Shaped like raindrops, they never moved. She never betrayed any emotion. When Jeffrey was depressed, Emily flashed her pouty lips. When he was angry, her alluring eyes put him in a trance. Praying to God to give him one more day with

Her, Emily sat available with her thirty-two inch bust. Whatever emotion Jeffrey experienced, Emily was there, always accessible and never criticizing him.

"Don't worry about it," Jeffrey said. Emily, dead still, she said nothing. Jeffrey turned to her, spooning the naked figure, he said, "I know what will make you feel better." Rolling on top of Emily, Jeffrey began kissing her naked body. Sliding his tongue down in between her breasts, Jeffrey kicked Emily's legs apart and slid into her.

On the steps in front of the house, just off the boulevard, William and Lena were talking. Explaining how he had broken down at the burglary, William said, "You need to talk to him."

"Me?" Lena said. Changing the subject, she said in an accusing manner, "What the fuck was that in there?" Accusing William of malice, she pushed him. The shove caused William to fall back a couple steps.

Regaining his posture, getting into Lena's face, William said, "You know I'm right, Lena!" His face close to hers, the warmth of his breath on her lips, he said, "Don't act like I'm not right!"

Backing away, pacing back and forth on the sidewalk, Lena looked up to the window of the master bedroom. A dim light from the lamp, she could make out a

Drama Dolls

shadow in the window. Up and down a dark head passed into view, disappearing suddenly.

When Lena returned to William, he was back in her face. "You need to talk to him," he said. Pointing his finger at her, he said, "This is what's best for him." William pleaded his case. His body deflated, exhausted from the continual heists and getaways.

Lena turned away. She was holding in tears. Her body began to shake and her heart started to beat faster. Looking back up to the bedroom window, a silhouette of an upper torso appearing, she burst out crying.

Sighing, William said, "Lena." He followed her gaze, stepping in front of her view, attempting to convince her. "Please tell me you will talk to him."

Covering her mouth with her hand, her eyes wet with tears, she fell to her knees and bawled. Moving her hands up over her eyes, her voice shaking as she spoke, Lena said, "I don't know."

William scratched the side of his neck. Spinning around, looking out into the darkness, William brushed his hand through his hair. Scratching the top of his head, he placed his other arm on his hip. William stood still, his back toward the crying Lena. Breathing in and out, slowing down his pulse, William closed his eyes.

A soft voice, his body calming, William said,

"Lena." Sniffling below him, Lena stared into the sidewalk. "Lena?" William said. He said, "Promise me you'll talk to him." Turning around to face the emotive cheerleader Doll, William looked down and saw the top of her head. "This is for the best."

Never looking up to him, still in a kneeling position, Lena nodded her head in agreement.

William craned his head up toward the bedroom window, looking into the faintly lit room. In the opening, shadowed cast from the lamp, showed two figures having sex. Staring for what seemed to be an eternity, William said, "We both know it."

He turned back to Lena, whose head was buried in her chest. "Trust me," he said.

Tiptoeing up each step on the staircase, the stairs creaking beneath her as she walked closer to the bedroom, Lena's breathing increased. Her heart was racing. The sounds from the room growing louder.

A sliver of light escaped from underneath the door. Its cheese wedge shape being interrupted by random shadows. Through the door, the bed frame was quietly squeaking. The casters digging into the floors. They were making small divots after a while.

Reaching for the decorative knob, Lena pulled

Drama Dolls

back when a loud groan filtered under the door. She slid down the wall, onto the hardwood. Sitting with her head buried into her knees. Her body started convulsing. Tears began to fall from her warm, damp cheeks.

"Emily... yeah... that feels good," coming from the room. Hearing Jeffrey's voice only made Lena worse. His wife had been gone for not nearly as long as her own spouse, yet he was coping better than she was.

The bed rocking increased, the divots formed by the casters rounding out deeper into grooves. "Uh... uh... oh... UH!"

The surround sound of love grunts echoed off the walls. Lena stared into her lap, her kneecaps saturated in sweat. The humidity in the house was uncomfortable. The polyester from Lena's cheerleader skirt was sticking to her thighs.

Pulling the fabric from her skin, releasing the sweat beads that were trapped underneath, Lena straightened out her legs and sat still. Listening to Jeffrey and Emily in the bedroom through the wooden door that separated them.

The phone rang suddenly, startling Lena. Leaning her head down to the floor, Lena peeked into the bedroom to see if Jeffrey was getting up. The bedframe's feet shaking repeatedly, the phone was ringing its third chime.

Jeffrey's voice, imperceptible under the loud drumming of the telephone, became audible when the answering machine turned on.

"Emily!" Jeffrey said. His voice, it was ethereal in the dark quarters.

Lena swallowed her tears, saliva in her mouth she had to take down before choking.

A woman's voice pouring out of the speaker was announcing to Jeffrey that she loved him and should call her soon. "We all miss Her," the disembodied voice said. "Please let me know you're OK."

Lena crawled into the spare room where the phone machine was. A blinking twelve enticed Lena to hear the messages. The twelve, flashing on and off, mocking her, invited her to push play.

A fingernail distance away from violating Jeffrey's privacy, Lena withdrew her arm and walked back into the hallway. She slinked down to her former position, the back of her thighs sticking to the floor.

The bed rocking louder, Jeffrey's grunts hollow against the walls, the lovemaking culminated when Jeffrey squealed, "UHH!"

Silence ensued.

Lena, lying flat on her chest, she peeped under the door into the master bedroom. A clicking sound scared

Drama Dolls

her back. Then, the cheese block of light vanished from under the door.

Alone, in the dead hush of the house, the only light came from a street light on the corner of the block. Illuminating another room in the home, the faint light shadowed Lena as she buried her head into the floor, attempting to recover. Her sniffles were short and quick. Cottonmouth in exchange for saliva. Her cheeks were balmy. They were becoming a sticky dryness.

Lena was picking Jeffrey up for coffee when she first met Emily. Entering his antique house, Lena was amazed at how beautiful the inside was. Staring up at the basketball-hoop-high ceiling, eying the crown molding around the perimeter, Lena's vision found the brick fireplace positioned in the center of the wall in the living room.

Everything flowed together nicely in the home. "Would you like a tour?" Jeffrey said.

Lena's eyes never met Jeffrey's, only tracing the entire outline of the interior.

After the fireplace, Lena focused on the inlays in the hardwood floor. The floor's design covered much of the entry way between the front door and the foot of the fireplace. Moving her gaze around the room, her eyes widening to the size of softballs, Lena discovered the decorative wall sconces that surrounded the doorway to the dining room.

Gas lights converted into electric, the light fixtures donned an ornamental design consisting of elongated faces with chins that curled back into the fixture. Covering the candle-shaped bulbs were fabric shades with fashionable beads hanging off the shades' skirts.

Clearing his throat, Jeffrey said, "Lena?"

A frozen smile on her face, Lena reached out to feel the dangling beads. "Wow," she said.

Jeffrey laughed.

Lena, turning to Jeffrey, her face still in an enraptured expression, said, "This is incredible."

"I can show you the entire house if you'd like," Jeffrey said.

The overwhelming feeling of how stunning the Victorian house was dissipated when Lena looked toward the couch. Sitting in a black gown by Adam Lippes was a dolled up Emily. Her complexion was flawless. Silver lip gloss made her pink lips glow. Eyes tempting, she was staring into nothing. Her blond hair, combed straight down, it was shoulder length, barely exposing her neck.

Drama Dolls

There was a glass of pink Moscato sitting on a coaster on the end table next to her. A silvery lipstick impression around the tumbler's rim.

Lena's expression changed suddenly. Going from elation to fear, she slow glanced over to Jeffrey.

"Oh," Jeffrey said, nonchalant. "Where are my manners?" Jeffrey bent down and collected Emily's high heels. He tossed them out of the way and said, "Please, sit." He gestured to the spot next to Emily.

Lena moved her eyes back and forth from Jeffrey to Emily.

"Lena, this is Emily." His arm extended, hand pointing toward the spot, Jeffrey said, "Please."

Tiptoeing past the RealDoll, Lena sat down on the couch. She made it a point to leave a good distance between herself and the life sized fuck doll. Reaching her palm out, her fingers close together, Lena shook Emily's hand. The softness of the phony hand surprised Lena. The aroma of Coco Mademoiselle stunned her. "Is that a Chanel?" she said.

Smiling, blasé in his demeanor, Jeffrey said, "It is! You sure have a nose for good scents." He said, "Would you like a glass of wine?"

Shaking her head, looking outside into the daylight, Lena said, "I thought we were going for coffee?"

Outdoors, the day was clear and the air was calm. A perfect day to venture out.

"Of course," he said. Looking over at Emily, he said, "You don't mind, do you?" The sex doll did nothing. She remained still and silent. Returning to Lena, Jeffrey said, "Well, let's go."

The pair exited the house, and although the introduction to Emily was forefront in her mind, Lena never addressed the issue that entire day.

Having cried until her eyes burned, Lena finally got herself together. Standing to her feet, she ran down the staircase light footed. Her swift movement enabled her to vacate the house without notice.

When she hit the pavement, just in front of the Queen Anne, she again began to cry. Her loud cries evaporated into the night sky. Her shoulders bouncing up and down as her body sulked to the point her chin fell into her chest.

Collapsing onto the sidewalk in front of Jeffrey's house, Lena sat with her legs crossed. The streetlight shining on top of her, Lena's shadow displayed a defeated cheerleader.

Drama Dolls

Closing her eyes, sockets collecting tears, she said, "I'm so stupid." Picking up a pebble and then tossing it out into the street, she repeated, "I am so stupid."

The shadow in front of her lengthening, its head extending up into the sky, Lena said, "Why am I so stupid?" She looked up into the clear sky, into the heavens, hoping that an answer would present itself. There was not a single star up above to wish upon, leaving Lena alone with her thoughts.

Peeking out from behind the curtain, Jeffrey watched Lena from his bedroom window. Emily was sleeping in the bed. Exhausted from the evening's activities. She had never been keen on the burglaries, always faking sick, or being tired, conveniently beforehand. The excuses Jeffrey made for her, they didn't always boil over well with William. He had been aggravated from the get go.

Faded weeping rose to Jeffrey's open window as he stalked Lena, pacing back and forth on the sidewalk. The grieving Doll's body grew tired by the second. Jeffrey watched Lena's mouth moving up and down. A conversation to herself, her gestures, they ranged from hands thrown in the air to palms smacking her forehead.

Jeffrey smiled at the sight. Lena had always been

there, ever since the two had met in support. One of the things that attracted him to Lena was that she never judged him. She always understood what he was going through. Lena always put him before herself.

Sleep deficiency was at its highest. A feeling of lightheadedness hitting him, the adult man cheerleader blinked his eyes. The batch of leaves in his view going out of focus, Jeffrey blanked out in his position.

After the initial awkwardness of talking about their dead spouses, Lena approached Jeffrey at the end of the bereavement support group meeting. Standing at the refreshment table, a water cooler between them, Lena introduced herself. "I'm sorry to hear about your wife," she said, extending her arm for a handshake.

Switching the paper cup to his other hand, Jeffrey reached out. He said, "Thank you. This has really helped." Behind them, loitering around in small pockets of people, were other grievers and supporters.

"Things will get better," Lena promised. Her husband had been gone for nearly a calendar's worth of days, and every day after was a test. She said, "It took me a long time. I didn't leave my house. I lashed out at my

Drama Dolls

friends, my family, anybody whose life was happy."

Jeffrey tilted his head, listening to his new friend. "When did you know you were going to be OK?" he said. "When everything would be fine?"

Grievers dispersed one at a time around them, leaving only a few still lounging around.

Shrugging, Lena said, "I don't know if I'm even at that point, yet." Looking at the remaining grievers in attendance, Lena smiled as a woman collected her belongings to leave. The woman waved to Lena and then receded out of the room. "Sure, I've moved on," Lena said, returning to Jeffrey. "I had to. But ever really feeling OK? I'm not sure I am."

The group leader waved to the general assembly, rotating left to right to include each person in the room. He vacated without saying good-bye.

Lena, waving without acknowledgement, said, "You have to find things that make you happy. People who support you. It's very important you surround yourself with positive people."

Moving in closer, the words making an apparent impact on Jeffrey, she said, "I would look at old photographs of when I was happy just so I could feel that way again."

A man tapped Lena's shoulder as he walked by

189

and waved. A big smile to his direction, Lena said, "See you next week." The man nodded and continued the trek to the door.

Refocusing on Jeffrey, Lena said, "There was a picture from back in the day where I was climbing on one of those indoor rock walls." Excited, able to share her stories with another person, Lena said, "I totally forgot about that day. So, you know what I did?"

Jeffrey laughed. He knew the answer, but instead of finishing her sentence, he said, "I can't imagine." A woman lurking in the corner listening in to the conversation triggered Jeffrey to acknowledge her and smile.

"I went out and rock climbed." An "aha" moment hitting her, allowing her to recapture that feeling again, she said, "That whole two steps forward, one step back saying? That definitely applies." Her hands in between them, animating while she confessed her life as if it was one dark secret, Lena said, "For me to move forward, I had to go backward first."

Waiting for a break in the dialogue, the woman lurking said, "Lena, I'm taking off."

Addressing the woman, Lena said, "Oh, OK." Lena and the woman hugged.

Turning to Jeffrey, the woman said, "Thank you

Drama Dolls

for sharing your story. I hope this group can help you move on."

Jeffrey, his memory jogging back to the session, lowered his eyebrows and said, "You're the realtor with the twin." Smiling in melancholy, the woman nodded her head. His eyes enlarging, Jeffrey said, "I didn't mean it to come out that way."

Her hands up, palms facing the new griever, the realtor said, "No, no, no. I know what you meant." Smiling with her teeth, she said, "I'm not offended. Once you've been here long enough, you'll realize that." Turning to Lena, the two women hugged again. This time, deeper, more meaningful. Lena, closing her eyes tightly, pulled the woman into her. The realtor started to cry. The crying turned to laughing.

Releasing each other and withdrawing, Lena holding the woman's shoulders, she said, "Take care of yourself." The woman wiped her eyes and nodded. Lena said, "I'll call you later."

The realtor smiled at Jeffrey, excused herself, and exited the room.

Lena, turning back to Jeffrey, said, "If you can find people who will support you, don't ever let them go."

191

Standing in his room, Jeffrey closed his eyes halfway and then opened them. His vision was going in and out of focus. The time elapsed without warning. Jump cutting through his brain.

His head swirling around, his neck began to ache from the sharp pulls and tugs of his head dropping. A jolt lifted his head up suddenly. Shaking his head, eyes blinking repeatedly, the fading of Lena walking back and forth gave Jeffrey a headache. Body fatigued, head falling back as his eyes closed, waning to black.

In and out of his head, Lena was saying, "For me to move forward, I had to go backward first." Visions fast forwarding from when She died to when he met Lena played underneath as the words, "For me to move forward, I had to go backward first," zipped through his mind. Flashing back to his childhood, his days in school, his teenaged life, all the way up to his current existence, Lena was saying how for her to move forward, she had to go backward first.

"For me to move forward, I had to go backward first." Echoing in his brain.

The inner Jeffrey, it was saying, "For me to move forward, I had to go backward first."

When Jeffrey came to full consciousness, Lena

Drama Dolls

was gone.

Tuesday:

A STICKY NOTE ON HIS computer screen saying COME SEE ME started off the work day. Being a controller for a manufacturing plant allowed Jeffrey to be tucked away in a corner office. The accounting team pushed to one side provided an intimate atmosphere separated from the rest of the company. This allowed for a much needed stretch of silence. Especially since Jeffrey had had only a few minutes of sleep in the last couple days.

The office's open area fit a pair of desks. One large secretary desk in the center of an alcove. Loretta had been an administrative assistant for all of her adult life.

Drama Dolls

Her retirement was counting down on her window saver's marquee for all to see. Each day, Loretta, she would change the date to reflect the countdown, uttering to nobody that she only had three years, fifteen days, twelve hours, and forty two seconds left.

"Forty one," she joked. Laughing to herself, she said, "Now, forty seconds."

An older woman, graying hair to her shoulders, Loretta inputted orders and then printed out papers for truck drivers to sign for pick-up. The printer was always shooting out pieces of paper. Her whole day was a cycle. A recurring cycle.

In between the data entry, Loretta would humor the truckers who flirted with her while their trailers were being loaded. Married herself, Loretta bantered back. "It's good customer service," she would always say.

Sliding the paperwork under the open slot under the glass divider, Loretta said, "Just need a signature, sweetie." Waiting for the trucker's John Hancock, she said, "Go ahead and pull in."

The trucker, smiling his toothless bottom of a mouth, said, "I'll go ahead and pull in."

Loretta smiled, laughing at the double entendre. She was always making the drivers feel at home.

The driver backed his twenty-foot flatbed into the

bay. Once in place, the fork trucks maneuvered around the semi. Picking up sheets of metal with their forks, the trucks loaded the large grades of steel onto the bed of the truck. Metal rubbed against metal, sending out echoes throughout the plant.

The driver, he was yelling into the window. Over the screeching of the steel, screaming toward the office window, the trucker said, "Have a good one, dear!"

Loretta smiled. Standing with a blank expression, she gazed out into the plant.

The other workstation belonged to Kelly, the accounting clerk, whose desk was enclosed in a single panel workstation. Her cubicle was near empty. The only thing hanging was a calendar with various days circled. A stack of paperbacks in the corner, her current read with a piece of cardboard she used as a bookmark.

Poking his head into the area to address his employees, Jeffrey said, "I'll be back." The Post-It, in big block lettering for all to see, was in between his fingers.

Without flinching, her fingers tapping away on the keyboard, Kelly nodded.

Before Jeffrey could get too far, Kelly said, "I almost forgot." Pulling out a piece of paper from the top drawer of her desk, she said, "Here is the recipe for your birthday cake I said I'd get for you."

Drama Dolls

Collecting the recipe in his free hand, Jeffrey said, "Oh. I didn't ask, but thank you."

"No big deal," Kelly said. Her attention zoomed in on the monitor, she said, "I brought it in yesterday but you didn't come in."

Eyes moving side to side, his mouth slowly opening, Jeffrey said, "I wasn't feeling it."

There was no response from his subordinate.

Drawing up an excuse from thin air, he said, "Didn't anyone notify you that I wasn't coming in?" When Kelly did not respond, Jeffrey dropped the conversation.

In the plant, through Loretta's window, there was a worker parking a fork truck into a stall. Loretta observed the operator, still peering into the industrial facility. "Loretta?" Jeffrey said. "I'll be back."

With no acknowledgement, her back toward him, Loretta waved her fingers in his direction.

Swinging back into his office, Jeffrey threw the recipe into the garbage can. He pulled out several tissues and then wadded them up and covered up the sheet of paper so that Kelly would not see.

Returning into the common area, sticky note in hand, Jeffrey announced, "I'll be back." Loretta and Kelly said nothing.

197

Walking through the plant, his cheerleader skirt blowing up against his legs as he passed each cooling fan, Jeffrey crossed a plant worker. The subordinate whistled at Jeffrey. He said, "Nice legs," and then he laughed.

The steel fortress, during the summer days, saw temperatures in the triple digits. Many loaders, they wore protective masks and heavy duty gloves. Covered head to toe in denim uniforms and steel-toe boots. Often times, the laborers passed out from the heat.

When the bodies collapsed, supervisors would drag the workers outside, laying them flat on their backs until they came to. After a dozen employees fell unconscious, the company stopped calling ambulances. A splash of water and some fresh air were enough to bring them back to life.

The controller passed the loading bays. In each bay were stacks of steel waiting to be retrieved by customers. The workers in their stations stopped as Jeffrey sauntered by. The heat made his legs sweaty. Perspiration dripping down the hair on his shins. Ankle socks were soaking wet, his white cheerleader shoes accumulating dirt on the bottoms. Careful not to touch any metal, Jeffrey did not want to dirty his uniform that he was so proud of wearing.

Fans bolted up in each section blew through

Drama Dolls

Jeffrey's skirt, giving each employee and truck driver a Marilyn Monroe moment they could write home about.

One trucker whistled. Another waiting for steel fired his air horn. The sound deafened the plant, ringing through the eardrums of each person. The note sticking to Jeffrey's finger attached itself to his earlobe when he plugged his ears from the loud horn.

Cutting a look to the trucker, Jeffrey noticed the driver laughing.

Continuing through the plant, Jeffrey ignored the expression on each employee's face. Each look alternated from shock to sneers. Mouths dropped open as Jeffrey passed; his focus was only to the front office on the opposite side of the plant. Usually he stayed hidden in his office, only associating with Loretta and Kelly. The rare times he was in the plant, it was because Jeffrey was getting clarification on a transaction. Or in this case, meeting with the head honcho.

The Russian Red lipstick began to run down his bottom lip. The black eyeliner dripped down his cheeks. Nose itching from the foundation caused him to wipe his face. Jeffrey's hand, smearing the makeup, it was now a dark bloody color. His face showed a smeared expression side to side. Smudged around his lips, black eyes spreading outward, Jeffrey's face was a slow motion scene caught in a photograph.

Venturing through the humid plant, Jeffrey still had a football field length to walk. The laborers whispered around him. Their laughs echoing through Jeffrey's head. They were bouncing off each other.

"Hey there baby!"

"How much?"

The hilarity, it was increasing.

"I got something for you!"

Jeffrey's knees got weaker. The dark eyeliner ran down his face like death tears. The sticky note on his lobe blowing as he passed each fan. Lightheaded from the extreme heat and lack of sleep, his face tingling from the makeup, Jeffrey became dizzy.

Metal being dropped by fork trucks into the stalls, the noise piercing his ears, Jeffrey started to slow down his gait. From the dizziness, he started to drunk walk the rest of the way. Wobbling periodically and taking each stride with one foot directly in front of the other as if he were walking a tight rope, Jeffrey pushed onward.

His forehead glistening a peach stain, the masculine cheerer wiped it dry with his wrist. A smeared peach color to match the rest of his tarnished face.

There was only a semitrailer distance left. Jeffrey's hair, it had expanded from the humidity. Ripping off the

Drama Dolls

wig, Jeffrey's real hair slicked back on his scalp, he ran the rest of the way. The Post-It note dangled from his ear, eventually flying off and floating down to his forearm.

Running full speed caused his skirt to float up in the air. Employees from afar, they laughed at the sight of the accountant's backside. One laborer whistled. Another screamed.

The brain of hair in his hand, Jeffrey brushed the note off of his arm. Floating into a corner, the sticky note was a feather falling to the earth.

Employees hollering from their work stations, their testosterone increased by the second. Their whistles and comments blurred through Jeffrey's mind. The truckers blew their air horns. And Loretta, she yelled out from the window, "You go, girl!"

Entering the air conditioned front office, a blast of cool breeze on his skin, the lipstick hardening before him, Jeffrey placed his wig on his head. Crooked, adjusting it on the fly, his face drying to permanency, Jeffrey knocked on his boss's door.

His eyes felt as if they had rolled back into his head but were looking straight on. A sharp pain in his forehead, the air freezing his face, Jeffrey stopped all action and closed his eyes. A brain freeze stunned him for a moment. The black of his inner eyelids in front of him, he could see transparent squiggly lines moving down the darkness. When the shrill sting passed, Jeffrey entered the office.

Greeting his employee, the boss said, "Jeffrey, have a seat." Jeffrey's skin shrinking from the cool air as he claimed a seat, the company controller pulled out his own chair and sat down.

Sitting in the chair, Jeffrey was face to face with his employer. The boss, the owner of the company, he had built the steel servicing center from the ground up. Awards for small businesses, excellence in service, they were framed on the wall behind him. A full page newspaper article featuring the company was professionally framed, hanging next to the awards.

The icy gusts of air, coupled with the coolness of the leather seat, gave Jeffrey goose bumps. Skirt riding high up his thighs, every inch of his legs was covered in pimples. His makeup was stiff like plaster.

The boss, his head tilted upward, looking down toward his accountant, said, "Jeffrey, I know you just lost your wife." The boss's stare locked onto Jeffrey. The gaze burning through Jeffrey's skull, the president of the company said, "So, I just wanted to see how you were doing." Squinting his eyes, his nostrils flaring, the boss

Drama Dolls

said, "Did you have a nice day off yesterday?"

The front of Jeffrey's wig facing toward the window, his real hair was seen in various spots. There were tiny bumps on his cheeks from the foundation hardening and then settling. Jeffrey's eyelids were now sticking to each other. Eyeliner smeared to his earlobes. His lips, they were a deep red.

Crossing his legs, thigh exposed, his knee was pasty white. Nodding his head slowly, he said, "I did. Thanks for asking." Adjusting himself on the chair, Jeffrey said, "As for how I'm doing? Well, nothing seems to be wrong." Focusing in on his boss, his eyes piercing, Jeffrey displayed a professional demeanor.

With his eyebrows lowering, the boss's attention moved to Jeffrey's knee. Moving up his skirt, eying the cheerleader sweater for a brief moment, the employer's focus drew to Jeffrey's face. "Are you sure you're feeling alright?"

Head shaking, the chill becoming unbearable, Jeffrey said, "Feel fine." His nipples pulling and twisting from the cold caused him to squirm in his chair. "No problems here," Jeffrey said, his voice an octave higher and cracking. "You don't have to worry about me." Attempting to compose himself, Jeffrey straightened his body.

For a moment, his posture was upright. However, the pain from his skin being yanked by the cold air triggered a high pitch squeal from his mouth. "Ahh!" The discomfort nearly pulled him off the chair. His butt sliding off halfway. Catching himself, flexing his calves, Jeffrey slid back up into his seat. "Why do you ask?" he said.

The air conditioner vent pushed out a breeze of freezing cold air, hitting Jeffrey directly into the face. Falling out of the chair, sliding down until the small of his back hit the edge, Jeffrey's knees crashed into the desk. "Oh my God!"

Patting down his chest with his palms, his nipples hard like Candy Corn, Jeffrey said, "I'm fine. Seriously." His face wincing from the pain of crushing the stiff nipples into his chest, Jeffrey said with his mouth and lips frozen still, "Really."

Standing over top of Jeffrey, behind the desk, the boss's arms out grabbing to help, he said, "Are you sure?" Reaching out, extending his hands, he said, "You don't look fine."

"I'm great," Jeffrey said, lengthening his body, returning to his position on the chair. "Totally."

Standing there with his hands up, reacting to Jeffrey's every move, the owner ensured all was well before sitting back down. "You're scaring the employees."

Drama Dolls

Concerned, his voice stern in delivery, he said. "Look at yourself."

Looking down, the skirt riding up his thigh, two pokeys coming from his chest, Jeffrey said, "What about me?"

Dropping his mouth, pausing for a brief second, the boss said, "You look like a transvestite Joker."

His heart was beating heavy. The freeze, not as impactful as before, was now suitable. "No, I feel fine."

"Go home," the boss said. "Take the rest of the day off."

Jeffrey, nodding his head, pursed his lips. "You sure?"

"People are complaining about you," the president said. He said, "Go ahead. Take another day for yourself."

Jeffrey and his boss had a brief stare down. With neither of the men caving in, Jeffrey said, "You want me to take another day?" Clearing his throat, he said, "Are you sure?"

The boss, staring at the employee who controlled all of the accounting functions for the company, the man who knew down to the cent how much was in the checking account, cash account, what the balance of the accounts payable and accounts receivable were, the person responsible for producing the month end financials for the bank and shareholders, and was now dressed as if a cheerleader got knocked up by a box of crayons, said, "This is an order."

Crossing his elbows, he said, "Now, go home."

The stoplight lasted an eternity. Windows were rolled down, the heat was beginning to melt pedestrians. Focusing on the bright red circle in front of him, Jeffrey heard the onslaught of deep bass approaching. The music getting louder, bass heavier, the voices attached to the sound became clearer. A soft hum of tires on pavement came to a halt.

In Jeffrey's peripheral, a carload of boys crept up to the line. The car's engine revving. The gas pedal going up and down. A four cylinder sedan imitating a Ferrari.

A clamor of laughter was coming from the back seat. Shotgun was occupied by a teenager wearing a sleeveless shirt. His right arm was covered in tattoos, a sleeve going down from his shoulder to his wrist.

Short blond hair, feathered, it was cut down and parted on the side. The boy, he was clean shaven. His eyebrows invisible.

His bare arm hanging out the window, he was tapping the side of the door. The tap-tapping and the music blaring weren't complemented. His fingers marching

Drama Dolls

to a different drum.

Louder and louder, the tapping continued. To the point his open hand became a fist. Arm flexed, his forearm defined, he was knocking the door hard.

Turning his head to address the boy, his cartoonish Barbie face in view with the teen's Ken facade, Jeffrey nodded his head down slow.

Without a reaction, stone cold demeanor, the boy raised his finger and then pointed it down the road. The light still red, on the opposite crosswalk, the countdown at 8, 7, the digitized numbers flashing on the screen, 6...

The sedan, revving until it came to the verge of dying, it sat ready in park. The boys in the back were falling over on themselves in amusement. The driver, he was preparing himself. Both hands gripped on top of the wheel. Eyes straight forward, he was standing by.

Ignoring the challenge, Jeffrey refocused on the red light. To the side, catching the remaining seconds, a woman walked her poodle. A cloud of a dog, shaved on his legs, he pranced alongside his owner.

The blond Ken, he pounded his door again. Short, loud thumps. Flexing his arm, the tattooed sausage of an appendage tightened, showing his triceps.

...5, 4...

The sedan gearing up, engine revving more and

more.

…3…

"Hey!" the passenger said out the door. He pointed out to the distance.

…2…

From the backseat, a boy, he said, "He a'int gonna race."

Craning his head back, the passenger laughed. He said, "Chicken."

…1…

Flooring it, the light changing from red to green, tires spinning, Jeffrey's Corvette accelerated through the intersection. There were black tire marks on the road. The sports car fishtailing at first.

Jeffrey eyed the rearview. The car shrinking as he extended the distance. Smaller and smaller it looked like a cinnamon roll in the middle of the road.

The poodle barking at the speeding car crossed the street with his owner.

Laughing out loud, the wind flowing through the Saran and Kanekalon, Jeffrey raced down the main street, heading toward Lena's. On the radio, Carly Rae Jepsen's "Call Me Maybe" escaped from the Corvette's Bose speakers.

Cruising around the town, taking every side road

Drama Dolls

possible to enjoy the free day off, the sports car handled well. Curving around a neighborhood street, a group of girls was jumping rope together. There was a younger boy sitting on the lawn with a toy truck. He was rolling it into the jump ropers, causing them to stop. A couple times they would chase the boy. Other occasions they would scream at him. He laughed each time.

Across the yard, the sprinkler churning water in every direction, toddlers jumped across the stream while others dodged the wetness. They yelled at the kids across the street, inviting them to come over. While the kids played, their mothers watered plants. Their fathers, they pushed mowers up and down the green grass, stopping to move gutter downspouts that were in the way.

The sun was shining bright. The day heating up.

Leaving the block, turning down another community, old ladies sat outside on a front porch. Rocking back and forth in chairs, they drank from lemonade glasses. The condensation running down the sides. Ice cubes shrinking in size, melting into the yellow drink.

A fenced in yard kept a dog from running amok. The black lab ran alongside Jeffrey's car as he drove by. The animal stopped when he could not go any farther. After he finished barking at the fleeing car, the dog stopped, turned around, and ran to the other side of the yard.

Building up speed Jeffrey exited the block, turning onto a main street. Blasting out of the speaker system, Madonna sang about dancing, for inspiration. "Into the Groove" starting on the radio resulted in Jeffrey turning the volume up. Singing along, Jeffrey braked at the next stop.

A car full of young women inched up next to his. Unaware of the audience, Jeffrey singing off key, the volume in his voice increasing, he belted the words to the tune.

The girls joined in. A redhead riding passenger filmed the scene with her phone. On her screen, in between the sing along, she giggled to herself. Her laughing made the phone unsteady. Narrating the video, the ginger said, "Ladies and gentlemen, if Medusa and a clown had a baby."

Jeffrey's face, it was covered in colored sweat. Artificial strands of hair intensifying from the humidity. His voice so awful it was summoning demons. A prostitute fetish clown driving a Corvette, belting out Madonna songs. That wasn't something you saw every day.

Leaning over the passenger seat, her head near the open window, the driver yelled, "You're sick!"

Drama Dolls

The redhead, phone still recording, turned to the driver, and said, "Isn't she fly?"

Singing loudly, Jeffrey's voice a beagle's bay, the words came out as a half-bark, half-howl induced a cappella diarrhea.

The freckled videographer laughing, her eyes in tears, she captured the event in high definition. Commenting over the music, she said, "OMG!"

Cars that had the green light passed in front of him. Whizzing through the intersection.

The karaoke escaped Jeffrey's 'Vette for those nearby to hear. He could see the owner of a mini-van in his rearview. She was falling back into her seat.

The backseat girls next to him, a brunette and blonde, they were screaming in joy. "Woo"-ing as Jeffrey's voice transitioned into an all-out yell fest. His voice cracking on the high notes.

The song ended. The light changed to green. And Jeffrey, this Drama Doll, was racing through the street crossing.

Sitting on her front steps, wearing a pink tank top, white shorts, and sandals, Lena painted her toe nails. Brushing the final nails, she looked up as Jeffrey pulled into her driveway. Her house, a small ranch with a single

Jason Tanamor

attached garage, was all she could afford after the bills were paid from her husband's death.

Starting over, training herself to be frugal, Lena was unable to find a steady job. She used the life insurance money to downsize. With both her and Jeffrey losing a spouse, the unlikely pair had found solace in each other's company.

The car sitting in park, the radio low, Jeffrey smiled out the window. His makeup had dried for the tenth time, smeared in all directions. His hair was nappy. Skirt riding up his ass, his lower butt cheeks sticking to the leather, Jeffrey leaned over the passenger seat to open the door. The adhesive compound that fused his skin to the seat made a ripping sound loud enough to cause Lena to flinch.

Entering the car, buckling her belt, she said, "That sounded like it hurt."

A pained expression on Jeffrey's face, his mouth frozen open, his eyes squinting in agony, he just sat and breathed heavily. His candy corn nipples had reduced to the size of pencil tips. Sharp number two pieces of lead that could fill in the circles of a Scantron wonderfully. The pain, it was still existent.

Lena said, "You look frazzled."

Back thighs burning, his face itching, hair

Drama Dolls

stretching in all directions like an octopus' tentacles, regaining himself, Jeffrey said, "I'm fine. No problems here." Moisture pouring out of every sweat gland, he said, "How are you?"

"I'm good." She flashed her fingers at him. "Look at my nails."

"Beautiful," Jeffrey said. "Totally."

She flashed her teeth, her lips curled upward. "Thank you," Lena said, holding out her hands in front of her to admire her work.

The car idling, the weather at its hottest, Jeffrey said, "What do you want to do today?"

Lena's smile slowly vanished. Sharply looking down at Jeffrey's chest, avoiding eye contact, she said, "We should talk."

The air between them became thick. The tension was starting to build. Turning the car off, Jeffrey said, "About what?" His voice, it became serious. His itchy nose irritated him. The lipstick tasted like paper. Swallowing hard, Jeffrey said, "What's this about?"

Adjusting her body to face him, Lena said, "I'm concerned about you."

"Why?" Jeffrey asked playfully, softening the conversation. Jeffrey's face was a spectrum of colors, soiled in every direction, mixing together to create new shades.

"Well," she said, her eyes open wide, "You look like you fell asleep in a bag of Skittles." A confused expression formed on Jeffrey. He was quiet. Waiting for a reaction, Lena frowned. She said, "William is concerned—"

"Fuck him," Jeffrey said, interjecting. "He doesn't want us to take Emily anymore."

A look outside, toward her neighbor's house, then up to the gutters on her own house, Lena, she was avoiding her friend.

Picking up on the gesture, Jeffrey said, "You don't want me to take her either, do you?"

She shrugged, her body pouting from the conversation. "Just think about it," she said.

"There's nothing to think about. Emily is a part of the Drama Dolls." Stiffening in his seat, entering fight mode, Jeffrey said, "What has she done to him? What has she done to you?"

Defensive, Jeffrey raised his hands up in front of him. His palms facing upward. "My wife just died for Christ's sake."

A crooked smile on her lips, Lena said, "I know she did." Reaching her arm out, Lena brushed her hand through Jeffrey's wig. The stickiness from the heat made it

Drama Dolls

difficult to run fingers through so after trying a couple times, Lena pulled back her hand. "I'm sorry," she said.

Jeffrey, his voice soft like a child's, said, "Can we still take her?"

Slow nodding in agreement, her eyes locking gaze with his, she said, "Of course we can." Seeing Jeffrey's face light up, Lena smiled. "You're right. She didn't do anything to us."

A change in attitude forced her to nod more sternly. Wiggling her toes, she said, "Look at my toenails."

Jeffrey and Lena had an afternoon's worth of time before meeting William for the evening's burglary. The two had decided to visit their loved ones' graves. But before that, Lena convinced Jeffrey to shower. She said, "You don't want your wife seeing you like this." Sniffing in his direction, she said, "Or, smelling like this."

Parking in front of Jeffrey's house, the cheerleaders walked up the flight of stairs to the Victorian. Next door, a Pontiac was parked in the street. The radio was playing and, inside, there were two bodies sitting in the front seat.

Looking into the side mirror, the shorter boy, smoking a joint, made eye contact with Jeffrey and nodded. Jeffrey nodded subtly, not wanting Lena to discover Jeffrey's joyride with the boys. In the passenger's seat, sticking his hand out the window, the neighbor boy flashed devil horns to the Drama Doll.

Lena, seeing the two fingers pointed to the sky, waved back.

"What're you doing?" Jeffrey said.

Lena, a dumbfounded expression on her face, said, "I don't know. He waved so I waved back."

Explaining the difference between a wave and devil horns, Jeffrey demonstrated. "This is a wave." Jeffrey put his hand up, widened his fingers, and moved it from left to right. "What the neighbor boy did was devil horns." His hand still in the air, Jeffrey bent down his two inside fingers, leaving just the pointer and pinky fingers extended. Thumb curled out away from the fingers, Jeffrey raised his hand and then head banged.

Sitting in the parked car, passing back and forth a joint to his friend, watching the demonstration in the side mirror, Alex said, "I told you he was fucking weird."

The shorter boy, inhaling on the drug, said, "Did you know he dressed up as a cheerleader for Insane Clown Posse?" Passing the joint to Alex, the shorter boy exhaled out the window.

Collecting the spliff, Alex said, "They're called

Drama Dolls

Juggalos." Joint in hand, Alex sucked in deeply. Holding in the pot until his eyeballs tightened, he said, "In the glove compartment of his 'Vette I found some makeup. There was lipstick, cosmetic case, you name it."

Returning the marijuana cigarette to his friend, Alex blew out the smoke.

His eyes halfway closed, his face melting, the shorter boy raised the joint to his lips. After he breathed in the drug, he pulled out the pot and rested the cigarette on the ashtray lip. Holding in the smoke, the boy said, "Yea. That is weird."

Spinning around to look out the back seat, Alex said, "But his girlfriend is pretty hot." Through the window, Jeffrey, standing on the porch landing, was head banging. Both of his hands now in devil horns, the adult cheerleader began jumping up and down simultaneously.

Lena, observing from her spot, followed suit. Forming devil horns with both her hands, Lena stuck her tongue out. Jumping up and down with Jeffrey, she banged her head in the air. Together, they were rocking out to a concert that didn't exist.

The shorter boy, taking another drag from the joint, he said, "She's weird too."

Inside the house, Jeffrey removed the Drama

Dolls uniform, throwing articles of clothing as he marched toward the shower.

Lena followed behind, gathering up the pieces as they were discarded on the floor. She pulled them close toward her, inhaling the scent of days with no sleep or showers.

The two separated, with Lena heading up the stairs to the master and Jeffrey hitting the bathroom.

Jumping into the bath, the water's temperature to Jeffrey's desire, he scrubbed his face with his hands. The water, it turned from a clear stream to a melting rainbow that circled the drain below. Closing his eyes, the water running down his face, Jeffrey took in the warmth.

The hot water was just what Jeffrey's body needed. He moved his body so the stream would hit the small of his back. Lena's kneecap during the pyramid was bony. Feeling the burn on his back made the pain subside.

Aching all around, sore from lugging heavy bags of jewelry and running down streets and woods, Jeffrey stood statue-still in the middle of the shower. The multicolored water turning clear, his body free from odor, Jeffrey felt refreshed.

Lena laid out the uniform on the bed, readying the outfit for the night's heist. There were sweat stains around

Drama Dolls

the skirt and cosmetics marks throughout the sweater. Licking her palm, Lena rubbed out the makeup stains. Saturating her hand with saliva, the female Doll rubbed the cosmetics until they disappeared from the white fabric.

Searching around the room for deodorant, Lena found a stick hidden behind the television. Removing the cap, she smelled the scent and then rubbed the stick on the sweat stains. Once the cheerleader outfit was as clean as it could get, Lena started to go through Jeffrey's belongings.

Walking around the room, situating items that she passed, Lena observed the movies by the television. Old classics lined up in a row; favorites watched during rainy days. *Gone With the Wind, Citizen Kane, On the Waterfront,* Jeffrey had them all. *Some Like it Hot, Ben-Hur, The Cincinnati Kid,* they all were snug in their cases ready for viewing.

There were musicals all around. *Holiday Inn, White Christmas, and Seven Brides for Seven Brothers.*

Lena smiled. Her collection was nothing of the sort. She was a simple girl who was happiest when she was married. Meeting Jeffrey had opened her eyes to a whole new world.

Peeking into the closet, clothing from Her still hanging, Lena flipped through the dresses individually, admiring the collection. Donna Karan, Alexander

McQueen, Anna Sui, and Badgley Mischka, they were all represented.

Shaking her head, Lena smiled. She wished she had an ounce of culture that Jeffrey and his wife had had. He was an accountant and she was a teacher. Yet, the two were always presenting themselves as if they were attending a White House dinner.

Moving from the closet, Lena approached the dresser. The room still had tangible memories scattered throughout. Old books, random photographs, jewelry in a stand, they all were signs of not letting go.

The water running below, Lena walked into a spare bedroom. Art purchased from different countries highlighted the walls. Collections of pieces acquired from various vacations. Furniture pieces shipped by air, they were dispersed around the house.

A matching bedroom set, the wood design the same on the bed as on the drawer as on the desk. The old houses were so beautiful to Lena. There was so much history. Restored from the inside out, it was no wonder how knowledgeable Jeffrey was with antiques.

Lena exited the room, turning the corner into another room. Along the back of the wall was a fireplace. On the mantel were miniature statues and figurines Jeffrey and his wife had found at estate sales or antique stores.

Drama Dolls

Some items had been brought back from Europe when they vacationed there.

The room was empty, used for reading. Set up like a museum. Lena leaned in to inspect a figurine. A foo dog statue, half a foot high, was sitting on a pedestal. Picking it up, Lena heard the shower stop.

Not wanting to get caught prying, Lena ran back to Jeffrey's room to collect his cheerleader uniform. Standing by the edge of the bed, Lena folded the outfit. With her feet underneath the bed, strands of hair tickled her toes.

Alarmed, Lena slid her foot back quickly. The force of her movement caused the strands of hair to slide out from underneath. Kneeling down, Lena flipped up the bed skirt and looked under the bed. Emily's blank face greeted her unexpectedly.

Screaming, Lena quickly covered her mouth and looked toward the hallway. Footsteps underneath her, she could hear Jeffrey walking closer. Curious, Lena slowly poked Emily's face. The realistic doll didn't move, her expression blank. Much like the cheerleader masks, Emily looked like a ghost.

Pulling her out to get a better view, Emily appeared bare naked. Sliding her around, examining the RealDoll's authenticity, Lena moved in closer to Emily's vagina.

She could not believe how genuine Emily was. Her heart sank. William was right. Jeffrey needed help. He shouldn't be bringing her anymore.

Footsteps grew louder, the feet walking up the staircase. "Lena," Jeffrey called out. "Are you up here?"

Lena whispered, "Shit!" and pushed Emily back under the bed. Patting down the bed skirt, flattening out the creased parts, Lena stood to her feet and grabbed the cheerleader outfit.

"Thought you'd be in here," Jeffrey said.

Spinning around, holding out the Drama Doll uniform, Lena was greeted by a buck naked, fully erect Jeffrey Doll.

Lena dropped the uniform. It unraveled on the wood floor in between them. Kneeling to pick it up, her eyes on Jeffrey's face, she slowly retrieved the attire and stood back up. "You're naked," she said.

Looking down at his boner, Jeffrey returned to Lena and said, "I guess I am."

Moving her eyes anywhere but down, Lena inched around him and walked out of the room. Yelling behind her, she said, "I'll just wait downstairs."

Admiring his erection, Jeffrey shrugged. "I guess I am," he repeated.

Drama Dolls

As Lena waited for Jeffrey, she paced back and forth in mid thought. Replaying the previous moments got her thinking. She knew Jeffrey needed help. But, was she truly helping him? The bereavement group members all shared their stories. Each had lost someone. They all coped in various ways. *Maybe this was how a person like Jeffrey suffered?*

Adjusting a throw pillow on the couch, Lena returned to pacing.

The pharmacist in the group had found God. A retail worker became depressed and isolated herself for nearly a year. And Lena, she took steps backward in order to move forward.

Everybody grieved differently. *Maybe William was right*, Lena thought. *But, then maybe, she owed it to Jeffrey to let him work through the pain in his own way.* Jeffrey, after all, had opened the door to a whole new world for Lena. He filled the void that allowed her to heal.

Sitting down in the middle of the sofa, Lena dropped her head down into her chest. Her hands on her forehead, Lena stared down into the area rug. Just as she was going to dwell on the situation again, Jeffrey appeared.

"I'm sorry," he said. Lena looked up at him. "About upstairs," he said pointing to the ceiling. Locking gaze with the petite cheerleader Doll, he said, "I haven't slept."

Nodding slowly, Lena began to stand. Helping her up with his hand, Jeffrey grasped her wrist and pulled her up the rest of the way. "If it's all the same," he said. "I'd like to forget everything that happened and get on with the day."

Lena smiled. Placing her hand on his shoulder, she said, "That's OK. We all mourn differently."

Flowers from the last visit were knocked over. Heavy gusts of wind whistled through the cemetery. Trees were leaning in the same direction. A photo of a young boy was pushed up against a tree trunk. A grave missing a possession. In the distance, a riding lawnmower bustled as it moved back and forth.

A sense of calm brushed over Jeffrey. Bending over to retrieve the vase, he replaced the old bouquet with a fresh one. Something that had been repeated since Her unexpected death.

Rubbing the back of his neck, kneeling down by the headstone, tears fell as his eyes softly closed. The red darkness from the sun hitting the outer lids of Jeffrey's eyes made him sleepy. Humming from the lawnmower grew louder. The noise forced Jeffrey's eyes open.

Drama Dolls

There was a faint sound of music escaping the operator's headphones.

A backward baseball cap covering his shoulder length hair, the young man's sideburns glinted from the heat. He was shirtless, wearing nothing but blue jeans and tennis shoes.

The cemetery was empty. Green hills with tombstones protruding out of them filled the area. A large family mausoleum stood bravely in the center of the green space. Roads intertwined around the entire cemetery, all connecting with one another.

Stopping the mower, jumping off its seat, the man retrieved the photo. He looked around the cemetery, a shift long chore to find its home. Skimming the width of the landscaping, with no luck, the employee folded the picture and placed it into his back pocket. The humming continued.

Breathing in, Jeffrey focused on the grave. Staring into the dates etched into the stone.

It had been almost six months since Her death. Jeffrey's life was still not back to normal. In fact, it was far from it.

Circling around a grassy mound, the lawnmower weaving in between family plots, the cemetery worker mowed a patch of grass that was off one of the roads.

Driving on the gravel until he could park near his shed, the man waved at Lena when he rode by. Offering up a smile, Lena returned to Jeffrey, remaining behind her friend while he paid his respects. Headstones in the dirt, some were falling over, slanting toward the ground. Others were new, the cement clean and the words legible.

Lena scanned the entire horizon. Knolls and windy roads were the focal points in the architectural design. The cemetery was so peaceful.

Since her husband's death, Lena's visits had declined. What once was a weekly appointment became a bi-monthly event. After she met Jeffrey, her spouse was lucky to see a presence every other month.

It wasn't that her husband wasn't important; rather, moving on was something Lena needed to do. Distracting her mind away from Him was a way to do that.

The heat still a nuisance, Lena fanned herself with her hand.

The sun made it difficult for Jeffrey to concentrate. The heat of its rays draining his energy. Kneeling in front of the grave, Jeffrey's hands clasped together, Lena noticed that he wasn't moving.

The man working the lawns was now weed whacking around the stones. Through the thicker weeds, he gunned the trigger causing the motor to whistle loudly.

Drama Dolls

The noise was loud and often distracting. Lena looked over to the worker's direction, watching him remove a field of weeds growing by the road.

As for Jeffrey, he remained motionless.

Turning her body so the sun didn't shine directly in her face, Lena stared at the spot where her husband was buried. Having promised Jeffrey that they would grieve together, the long prayer was beginning to get on her nerves.

The hum of the weed whacker increased, drowning out any other noise within shouting distance. Lena plugged her ears. Jeffrey, again, stayed still. His head into his chest, hands clasped, kneeling into the grass.

How can you not hear that? Lena thought.

When the man attacked a patch of weeds by the stones next to them, Lena walked over to Jeffrey and placed her hand on his shoulder. Tipping over, Jeffrey fell over onto the grass. His eyes were closed and there was a smile on his face. The sun shining upon him, Lena could tell he was sleeping.

Lena waved to the man working. When he didn't respond, she ran over to him. Her sandals flopping underneath her, she said, "Hey, my friend likes to take naps by his wife's grave as a way for him to sleep next to her." Pointing over to Jeffrey on the ground, she said,

"Would you mind keeping an eye on him while I visit somebody on the other side of the cemetery?"

The cemetery worker, looking across the green space, shrugged his shoulders. "Sure thing."

It took three large hills and two road intersections to reach her husband's gravesite. Sitting cross-legged in front of the tombstone, Lena said, "Hi Danny."

The etching on the stone read LOVING HUSBAND AND BEST FRIEND. Weeds were growing around the grave and to avoid an interruption, Lena pulled the weeds out and threw them off to the side.

Speaking into the headstone, Lena said, "I'm sorry I haven't been around. It's not that I don't miss you, it's just that it's too hard for me to deal with." Sniffling, her body getting weak, she said, "I brought my friend Jeffrey. You'd like him. He's fun. He's an accountant."

She laughed. "I guess that sounds funny." Shaking her head, she said, "A fun accountant?" Looking in the direction of the sleeping Jeffrey, she said, "But really. He's great."

Extending out her legs, Lena kicked off her sandals. Wiggling her toes, she said, "I painted my nails your favorite color." A teardrop formed under her eye. Another soon after.

Drama Dolls

Scratching some dirt off the tomb's dates with her fingernail, Lena said, "I can't believe it's been a year and a half since you died."

The sun beginning to set, the air still warm, Lena laughed and cried at the same time. "I think you'd be proud of me." Twisting her ankles, her feet moving in a clockwise rotation, she said, "I learned how to downsize and not live beyond my means." There was nervous laughter. "Not that I blame you for not teaching me. Why would you have? You gave me everything a girl could ever want."

Standing to her feet, stepping up on her tiptoes, Lena looked to where Jeffrey was sleeping. Seeing that he was still passed out, she dropped to her knees. "My life is completely different now. I'm learning about old houses, crystal, I even went to a baseball game," Lena said. A short laugh escaped her mouth. "I know, I know. You always told me to have an open mind."

Pouring her heart out to her deceased loved one, she said, "I'm sorry I didn't experience these things with you. And I really don't know why I enjoy doing these things now." Her eyes straying from the gravesite, moving toward the openness of the cemetery, she said, "I blame Jeffrey."

Swallowing, the pent-up saliva disappearing down

her throat, she said, "You'd be amazed if you saw me now." A nervous laughter escaping her, Lena sat back down on the grass. Crossing her legs, she said, "Would you even find me attractive anymore?"

Lena's husband, for the better part, was a white-collar executive who worked late hours and traveled the bulk of the year. His down time was spent golfing with his friends. He allowed Lena to buy whatever she wanted in order to keep her happy. Lena never once thought he was taking her for granted, but now, having met Jeffrey and William, she was beginning to realize what she had been missing out on.

The couple never had children. Partially because Lena wasn't ready. He passed before she could ever change her mind.

Crossing her arms, Lena rocked back and forth. Silenced, she then placed her hands on her legs. Unable to get comfortable, and to reduce her nervousness, Lena began pulling on grass next to her. Keeping her fingers occupied calmed her nerves. The grass falling next to her as she pulled the blades out from the ground, Lena's attitude started to lighten. The smell of the greenery mixed in with the atmosphere relaxed her.

Her body lifting in excitement, she said, "Oh my God. I forgot to tell you. At the baseball game, Jeffrey

Drama Dolls

caught a homerun ball." Raising her arm high, pretending that she caught a ball, she said, "It was sooo cool. I didn't see it because I was hiding behind him." Pulling her arm down, Lena said, "But the entire stadium did. We were on the big screen for everyone to see." Smiling, her eyes became glossy from sharing the experience.

Removing the sweat from her forearms, Lena wiped her hands on the grass. She said, "I also met a man named William. He's a trip as well. The three of us hang out together regularly."

Her eyes moved left to right. Puckering her lips, forming a crooked smile on her face, Lena said, "I don't want you to be mad at me for not coming that much." A steady stream of tears down her cheeks, she said, "I will try to come out more often to see you." Her face soaking wet, she said, "I promise."

The weed whacker approaching, interrupting her moment briefly, Lena craned her neck to the direction of the motor. In her peripheral, she noticed Jeffrey was gone.

Standing, Lena pirouetted to find Jeffrey behind her. "Hi," she said. Sincere in her words, she said, "You were sleeping over there so I—"

Butting in, Jeffrey said, "You don't have to apologize." Pausing so the cemetery worker could pass by, he said, "I know you miss him. I'm sorry that we had to meet because our spouses died."

Sighing in relief, Lena said, "Danny would've liked you. William? Not so much."

Smiling, his eyes half closed from the bright sunshine, Jeffrey said, "C'mon. I'll take you home."

The two walked the long stretch toward Jeffrey's car. Both grievers were lost in their thoughts. Lena's mouth curled into a grin as she walked side by side with Jeffrey, who was staring blankly toward the parked automobile.

Passing by a family plot of gravestones, the couple arrived at the 'Vette. Once inside, the pair quietly drove off, never speaking the entire ride back to Lena's house.

Arriving at the residence, pulling into the driveway, the Drama Doll said, "I'll see you in a few."

It could have been the afternoon in the cemetery with Her that caused Jeffrey to feel better than usual. Spending the day with Lena was always nice as well. Especially without William. Clearing up the Emily situation was also a breath of fresh air.

Sitting behind his vanity, staring into the mirror, Jeffrey observed his face. Turning his head left to right, his face clean and free of makeup from the shower, he could see the wrinkles around his eyes becoming more prevalent.

Drama Dolls

Sun spots on his forehead, Jeffrey felt his age hitting him. Still a bit sore from the continual heavy lifting and non-stop action, the days of his youth were passing by.

Dressing up as a cheerleader still fulfilled him. To say that breaking into houses was as fun as when the Drama Dolls first started, that was not the case. It just appeared as if the same break-in was occurring each night. Pilfering the same types of jewelry, escaping down a similar path to freedom, and sorting through similar kinds of bracelets, necklaces, and earrings.

The voice of quality reason, silent for a while now, it was missing Her deeply. Visiting the gravesite only made it miss Her more.

Spotting the unraveled cheerleader uniform on the floor through the mirror's reflection, Jeffrey smiled inside. The excitement building for the night's heist brewing underneath his bitter exterior. Pumping himself up for another evening with his friends, Jeffrey breathed in heavily and then exhaled through his mouth. Pounding his chest like a gorilla, his lips smoking an invisible cigar, Jeffrey rose to his feet and grabbed his Drama Dolls outfit.

Sliding into the uniform, Jeffrey picked up his pom-poms and shook his wrists, fluffing the plastic stream of feathers.

In full getup, the adult cheerleader kicked his leg

up high into the air. A pom-pom in each hand, his fists on his hips, Jeffrey alternated kicks into the air. Skipping in place, building into a rhythm, the Drama Doll's theme song played into his brain.

Underneath the cloud of thoughts, the volume increasing as the music played, Jeffrey's chorus of his current life rang into his ears.

Raising up a pom-pom to his mouth, using it as a microphone, Jeffrey sang the lyrics to "I Will Survive" into the vanity's mirror. His reflection returned an uplifting image, an impression of hope that everything will be alright.

Jumping into a scissor kick, Jeffrey landed on his healing ankle. His ankle twisting awkwardly. The discomfort caused him to fall over onto the wood floor.

A record needle pulling off the groove, the music in his head stopped suddenly. Groaning in pain on the hardwood, Jeffrey grabbed his ankle and rubbed it.

The inner voice of sympathetic reason, it said, "Survive! Survive!"

Inside, Jeffrey was changing. He was feeling his age. Emotions still running wild, there was a different sensation. Jeffrey, he was accepting the situation.

Drama Dolls

Sneaking into the window near the side entrance, Barb entered first. She turned, waved Brittney in with her fingers. Instead of getting her partner, Emily appeared, arms extended.

"Seriously," Barb said. "You're bringing her?"

"What do you want me to do with her?" Brittney said, urging Barb to grab the body.

Frustrated, Barb said, "I don't know. You could leave her outside."

"Just grab her."

Annoyed, pulling the mannequin in through the window, Barb said, "Hell, you could've left her at the house." Barb heaved Emily up to her feet and propped her up against the wall.

Sliding in, Brittney followed. Looking at Barb, pulling Emily in close, Brittney said, "See? That wasn't so hard."

With Emily in tow, Brittney scaled the flight of stairs, lugging the RealDoll behind her. A slow trot, Emily's legs were dangling and her feet were kicking into the spindles of the railing.

CLUNK, CLUNK, CLUNK.

Barb was gaining distance on Brittney. Taking two steps at a time, she was already on the second floor. By the

235

time Brittney reached her, she had already taken down an entire jewelry stand of goods. Clip-on earrings followed large hoops followed butterfly rings. Dumping drawers into the pillowcase, Barb didn't care what she was taking or what the value was.

Dressed in a cheerleader outfit to the tee save for her mask, Barb still looked beautiful. When the two first met up for the heist, Brittney had inquired about the mask and Barb said, "I forgot."

"How you forget to bring your mask but still dress up is beyond me," the voice of detective reasoning said.

While Brittney perched Emily up against the wall, Barb continued to work. Emptying each drawer, each treasure chest, she gathered. Once meticulous, Barb rushed to unload the contents into her bags. Turning over drawers and then dropping them to the floor. Every opportunity Barb had, whether it was turning in front of the passed out Drama Doll or walking past her, Barb made a look.

As Brittney positioned her pillowcase to join Barb, Emily slowly slid down the drywall. Skirt hiking up the back of her, her clothing chipping the paint, she collapsed to the ground, falling over into a horizontal television stand. The flat screen tipped over, crashing onto the hardwood floor.

Brittney, running over to Emily, dropped her bag

Drama Dolls

of loot. "Oh my God, oh my God, oh my God!"

Barb, her neck whipping around to investigate the commotion, she said. "What the fuck?" Seeing the crashed electronic on the floor, Barb said, "Look at what you've done. There's fucking glass all over the floor."

Panicking, Brittney pulled Emily up and propped her up again. Turning to Barb, she put her finger up to her mouth, her lips pursed. Whispering "SHHH!" Brittney froze. Looking around to see if anyone was coming, she whispered again, "Shhh!"

Chattering outside stopped Barb short. Two kids, they stood outside smoking pot. The marijuana was coming into the window. Strong gusts filled the bedroom. In the dark, the cloudy fog began to surround Brittney and Barb.

Barb, she whisper/screamed, "Be fucking careful!" Peering out into the darkness, she said, "There are people outside."

Replacing the television on the stand, the screen shattered from the fall, Brittney moved to the corner nightstand. Pulling open the lone drawer, Brittney's eyebrows raised. There was a treasure trove of miscellaneous gems. Old watches and tiaras that were later replaced with newer items had found themselves stored away and forgotten.

There was a crash behind the Drama Dolls. Emily's head was now face planted into the floor. Her body in a downward dog position, her cheerleading skirt flipped over her ass.

Barb sighed, her patience tested. The looting ceased.

Laughter entered the room, coming from the kids outside. The smoke, filtering into the room as well, was now consuming Brittney's brain.

Dropping her bag, Brittney threw Emily up on the bed. Her neck craned to the left, her waist twisting to the right. Her legs open wide like scissors. To Barb, Emily was an artificial pretzel.

Ensuring Emily was in place, Brittney said, "Sorry."

Headlights passed through the bedroom. The glow stopping on the ceiling, then fading into darkness. A door slamming enticed Brittney to look out the window. There was another friend outside.

Staring in the direction of the voices, only catching a glimpse due to the way the roof pointed, a smile brushed over her. Brittney reminisced about the joy riding with her neighbor and friend. The drive made her feel youthful again.

The smoke, now in Brittney's lungs, was getting

Drama Dolls

her high. Underneath her mask, the sclera of her eyes turned a veiny red. Her head getting light, feeling suffocated from the mask, Brittney was breathing in and out of the hole for a mouth.

The kids, they conversed, yelled in delight, and laughed at each other's jokes. With the new addition joining them, the pitter-patter of voices became clear.

"When we meeting up with the girls?"

"After we hit this," one boy said, referring to the weed.

"And the girls?" another boy said.

The one with the pot, he said, "We're gonna hit it too."

Then there was laughter. Passing around the joint, they each inhaled deeply, their bodies becoming relaxed.

Clearing her throat, stretching out the rumbling inner burp, Barb glared at Brittney.

Brittney's hollow expression turned to address the Drama Doll. She was welcomed by an angry look. "Sorry," Brittney said.

Staring at Brittney, Barb's eyes pierced through the plastic mask.

"Sorry," the delusional cheerleader said again. "No more fucking around."

The duo continued with the burglary, filling bag

after bag after bag with all kinds of possessions. They weren't just packed with jewelry anymore. Anything of value, Brittney stole.

Barb, though, she had other plans.

Picture frames shoved into pillowcases, the glass breaking on one in the process. Half-filled lotion bottles, perforated condom chains, DVD remote control, anything that could be stolen easily, was.

Barb pulled out pajama bottoms from the dresser, a woman's size, petite with cartoon characters splattered on them, and shoved them into her bag. Mismatching socks were lifted. Anything that she could grab, Barb did.

The anxiousness started to bother Brittney.

Old magazines, they were rolled and slid into the sides. Entertainment magazines showing couples divorcing, car publications with models on the hood, an outdated *TV Guide*.

A lemon scented candle, almost at the end of its life, lifted for no particular reason. Seeing the pillowcases being filled at a rapid pace, Brittney said, "Be more selective!"

Car doors opening and then closing, ignition starting, the three buddies fled the scene. The cloud of marijuana smoke dispelling in the air.

Barb stopped all motion, her back toward Brittney

Drama Dolls

as she held a bag in her hands. Dropping the goods, she pirouetted, her white tennis shoes stomped into blue jeans. "Excuse me?"

"We're only here to take the valuables," Brittney said. A brief stare down ensued. "In and out. That's the plan."

On the bed, sprawled out like a dead body, the passed out Drama Doll separated them. Barb, she said, "In and out?" Gesturing to Emily, she said, "But you bring *this* thing?"

Defensive, her body clenching, Brittney said, "You take that back!" Breathing in and out, heavy breaths, they filled her lungs. A contact high hitting her, she said, "Take. It. Back!"

Pointing her finger to the ceiling, accusing Brittney, Barb said, "You, my friend, need fucking help." Then she left. A pile of a mess on the floor, shirts mixed with socks mixed with hairbrushes. Bags were falling down and emptying.

"Take it back!" Brittney screamed. Her head getting dizzy, the weed was enveloping her.

Barb's footsteps receded down the staircase. On the wood, her stomping was getting louder and louder. Steps in a straight line. The front door opened. Then it slammed.

"Take it back," Brittney whispered, her eyes now pink and watery. "Take it back."

Standing in the darkness, Emily on the bed, Brittney broke down in tears. Sinking to her knees, her hands covering her face so Emily wouldn't see. Pieces of clothing were scattered everywhere. The television shattered on the stand next to Brittney. Screams exited her body.

"FUCK YOU!" Echoing down the halls.

"MOTHER FUCKER!" Bouncing off the walls.

Hysterical, the tears were a garden hose shooting out of her eyes.

"BARB!" Screaming in the dark. "BARB!"

Drawers were pulled back from the walls, crooked in spots. The vanity was cleared and empty. Makeup bottles were on the floor. There were books everywhere. Bags filled with goods, crumpled down on the wood.

Crying on the hardwood, Brittney's body was shaking uncontrollably.

The shooter who took Her life also took his own. Barricaded in the classroom, his classmates hiding under their desks, crying, they were praying to see tomorrow.

Drama Dolls

The shooter's barrel pointed at Her head. A strong woman, protecting her students from the gunman, she offered up herself when the shooter's plan became compromised.

Sitting in a chair at the front of the classroom, with police surrounding the school and more outside the room in the hall, She begged him, saying that he could get help. That he could change his life. Could make it better.

"What do you know about me?" he said, his arm stiff in the direction of the teacher. "Your life, Mrs. Taylor, is perfect."

Picking up the framed photo on her desk, a married couple smiling in the center, the shooter said, "Look at you. Mister and Missus Taylor. A perfect couple." Grazing his thumb across the honeymooners' faces, he slammed the photo frame onto the classroom floor.

Students ducking under their desks, their heads buried into their chests, they muffled their cries to avoid attention. A scream coming from a girl under a first row desk. Tears down her cheeks, her face red, she weeping uncontrollably.

Turning to address the student, the gunman, he said, "Shut the fuck up!" He pointed the gun toward her. The teenager cried louder.

Desks shifted, the metal legs scraping on the floor, moved to furnish more protection. A couple desks fallen over, the tabletop used as a shield.

Jeffrey's wife, she kept her cool. Her body calm, relaxed, not displaying any emotion that the shooter could use. Adjusting herself on the chair, the leg scratching the floor, she again was faced with a barrel to her head.

"Don't move," he said. His body shaking, he looked out at the lineup of police men ready to shoot. A voice from the hall, through the door that separated the classroom, asked him to surrender. It said, "Let them go and turn yourself in."

The shooter, he started to pace, never taking his aim off Her. Back and forth, a few steps one direction, several more the other, he scratched his forehead with his free hand.

A boy, he poked his head up slow, surveying the scene. His gaze to Her, the shooter, and then to his fellow students. Mouthing words to himself, he closed his eyes tight, praying that the nightmare would end.

"We have the building surrounded," the voice said. "Let the hostages go and surrender yourself."

On the lawn, an officer waved to a policeman, motioning him to proceed.

Running to the window, the shooter watched the

Drama Dolls

policeman move toward the school. Another followed. Then another.

Students hiding, their eyes followed the shooter as he moved from the window to Mrs. Taylor.

"We are counting to three," the voice in the hall said, "and then we are coming in."

Walking in a circle, his gun in the air, the shooter pointed to the ceiling. He returned his aim to the teacher, back to the ceiling, and then to the floor.

All of this transpired while Jeffrey was at work. The news broke live to the scene. Loretta, she told her supervisor to turn up the radio. Every station, radio and television, broadcasting the ordeal. "Isn't that Emily's school?" she said.

Sitting together, Jeffrey and Loretta listened to the reporter describe the scene as it unfolded. Calling Her on the phone, ringing and ringing, Jeffrey listening to the news girl as she said that at least twenty people, one teacher, were being held hostage.

The reporter, broadcasting through the speaker in the office, said, "Police have surrounded the school. As many as fifty officers, their weapons drawn, are in place."

At the school, the voice said, "...3." The door kicked open, officers in position. Their guns were pointing toward the gunman.

Two shots.

One into Emily. The other into himself.

Students screamed out loud, the desks moving so they could escape. The shooter collapsed on the floor, his head hitting the tile. Blood trailed out of his skull, flowing into a puddle.

Emily Taylor fell over in her chair, her body crashing down, her brain splattering the wall and desks nearby.

The reporter said a shot was heard. "We'll bring you more on this story as details come in."

The silence was an eternity.

Loretta, calming Jeffrey down, she said, "It may not be her. They probably moved everyone to safety."

Coming back on the radio, the reporter, she said, "This just in."

Students ran out of the school. Screaming, crying, their hands covering their faces. The line of policemen entering the school as ambulances arrived on the campus.

"The gunman and a teacher, whose name was not released, are dead from single gunshot wounds. Eyewitnesses said that a shooter, who was also a student at the high school, entered the classroom and held the teacher hostage."

Helpless, screaming at the radio, Jeffrey dialed Her

Drama Dolls

phone.

"Students hid under their desks in fear as police officials talked the gunman into coming out. When he did not comply, police officers rushed into the classroom. The result was a murder suicide. Live here at the scene, I'm—"

Loretta turned off the radio. "They said they're not releasing the name, I'm sure, until the family is contacted."

Heart beating, panic building, Jeffrey breathed in and out. Calming down, his eyes closed, he could feel his body coming to a rest. Nodding his head, buying fully into Loretta's reasoning, Jeffrey opened his eyes.

Then, his cell phone rang.

"Hello?"

Jeffrey's life used to be something. Without her it became nothing.

Lena pulled around the alley. The getaway car filled will bags from prior heists. There were always bags full of jewelry. Barb/William was the only one waiting.

The alley was an aroma of discarded meals. The smell of egg rolls over sweet and sour in the air. Thick gravy poured into the dumpster, spilling down into the

247

bottom of the trashcan. The birds, they were eating rice and then flying away. A bum sleeping against the wall, he rolled over and covered himself with his blanket.

William was standing alone, looking back toward the botched burglary.

And Lena, she was saying, "Where's Brittney? Where's Jeffrey?"

Hopping into the passenger seat, William said, "He's still back there. He's fucking crazy!"

"What do you mean he's still back there?" she said. Dressed in cheerleader garb, Lena addressed Barb's face. "Where the fuck is your mask?"

William looked straight out the window. He was silent.

"You knew he was on edge!" Leaning in close to William, pulling off her disguise, she said, "Unpredictable!"

William, never looking at the getaway driver, said, "Just fucking go!"

Frantic, her mind running amok, Lena said, "Where's—"

Interrupting, William said, "Go!"

Driving back to the scene, the same route as before, through the historic district of houses, with balustrades wrapped around the front porches and towers shooting up toward the night sky, Lena said, "Why isn't he

Drama Dolls

with you?"

Bus stop signs passed, the bases littered with fast food containers. A multi-unit house, half of the residents awake by the living room illumination through the curtains. A blinking yellow light from the television played a program. The rest of the complex, the residents were dreaming until the next shift of work.

Rocking back and forth, tapping his foot, William said, "I'm guessing you talked to him."

The speed of the car increasing, bags of gems falling over each other with every turn, Lena sat quiet. Her hands were on the steering wheel, gripping so tight her fingers were numb. The escape vehicle rushed toward the house.

"Did you talk to him?" William said, calmly.

Lena's lip curled downward. Sniffling, she nodded. "Um hmm."

"You told him everything?"

Her head nodding in short, quick motions, she sniffled. "Yes."

"Everything?"

Her face turning red, tears fell down Lena's cheeks. The car jerked to a stop. A pillowcase toppled over the back seat, onto the floor. Various bead, wheat, and byzantine chains spilled onto the floor mats. Bangle bracelets followed. Tiaras were rolling off the seats. Pins sliding to the floor. Brooches displayed themselves.

"Lena!" William said.

Crying, weeping, her head buried into her knuckles on the steering wheel, she said, "I'm sorry!"

"You're part of the fucking problem!" William was screaming. The "loot" in the backseat was going in between the cushions, rolling underneath the front seats.

"This is all your fault!" William said. Breathing in heavily, he said, "I can't believe you talked me into such a bonehead plan!"

"I'm sorry!"

"You're sorry?" William said. "This was the dumbest— "

Her face covered in tears, Lena said, "I'm sorry!" Sniffling, she said, "I'm sorry! Stop yelling at me."

The story of the jewels, they were bought by Lena as a stay at home wife, packed together in pillow bags and brought to each scene.

"I'm an idiot for actually agreeing to this bonehead plan!" William said. Shaking his head in disgust, he said, "Un-fucking-believable."

The jewels, they were stacking up in the spare bedroom. Making it look as if multiple heists were taking place, Lena, she had schemed up a plan to "help" the

Drama Dolls

sickness. Help the healing. Help her friend.

Pacing around the room, gauging her surroundings, Brittney turned on the television. Pushing play on the DVD player, Bing Crosby singing "White Christmas" on the screen, her life was becoming surreal. Huddled in the center of the spider web of cracks, the holiday movie calmed Brittney down.

One of Brittney's favorite things to do with Her was watch Christmas movies. The winter holiday, Brittney's favorite, always made the couple feel grateful. Grateful for each other, the lives they were able to live, and the fact that they were both healthy.

The season was magical for the couple. Coming in quickly, only to exit as fast. Much like Her death, and Brittney's grief afterward, the cheerleader's reality had the same feeling of Christmas.

Emily passed out on the bed, sleeping because she was tired, she was always tired, Brittney pulled out the porno stash under the bed. Shuffling the movies aside, she grabbed the Pink Lady Fleshlight and untwisted the cap. Pulling down her panties, lifting up her skirt, Brittney serviced herself to Rosemary Clooney.

On the screen Bing Crosby was talking to Rosemary Clooney.

The answering machine blinked new messages.

"Your father is worried about you," and "Why don't you come over for dinner?" Unreturned calls from Brittney/Jeffrey's parents.

There were new messages from the realtor. "Please call me back," Jane said. "There is an offer on the house." Jane, the realtor, a bereavement group attendee, her twin brother had passed away. Helping Jeffrey was helping herself was helping Lena. After each "burglary," Jane and her assistant would enter the house and clean up. Rearranging the bedroom and putting it back together again. She convinced herself that keeping the house orderly would assist in the house selling faster.

Standing on the front porch, the sound of the movie sifting out the window, the television's alien light flickering into the night, William, he said, "You're feeding into his sickness!"

Defensive, attacking back, Lena said, "You're trying to sabotage him!"

"I'm trying to help him!" William said. Anger in his face, his eyebrows lowered, William was standing stern in full cheerleader getup. "He's fucked up! Can't you see?"

Lena's face was red from crying. Her throat was sore from screaming.

Drama Dolls

"When Jane was showing you the house, what do you think I was doing upstairs?" William said. Lena shrugged. Her was body quivering. "I was fucking cleaning the God damned house!" William said. "With Jane showing the house, she didn't have time to clean it herself!"

Pacing, his mouth filling with spit, William said, "All so we could rob it again!" Fuming, breathing heavily, he said, "Now, you on the other hand."

"I can't help it!" Lena said. Breathing out all of her emotion onto William, she said, "I'm in love with him!"

A gunshot fired up above.

The television blared out old movie lines.

The light, blinking on and off as the scenes transitioned.

Lena crying, she said, "Jeffrey!"

In his bedroom, Jeffrey's body was slouched in a pool of blood. Emily the RealDoll by his side. The black styrofoam hand, it sat bare on the vanity. Clothes in the closet were gifts for his wife. She would wear them on special occasions.

The inner voice, singing softly as the final breaths escaped it, *"When the music's over. Turn out the lights."*

The RealDoll box stashed in the closet, the price

just under five grand, it was a substitute when She passed. The box was filled with a cotton bag, a wig, and scented powder.

Emily Doll was wearing the wedding gown. The dress was stowed away in the attic's closet. A high-wasted empire gown that cuddled the figure with an extra-long skirt that concealed her hips. Emily's expression, her body's demeanor, willing to be used and abused however one pleased. One hundred percent guarantee or your money back.

On the RealDoll's finger was the wedding ring from the black velour hand.

Tipped over on the night stand was the bottle of anti-depressant pills. It was prescribed by the pharmacist from the bereavement group.

Morrison's voice, a ghost inside the inner Jeffrey, singing, *"When the music's over. Turn out the lights."*

Jeffrey, he was almost naked. His panties were down around his ankles and the Fleshlight was between his legs. The black semiautomatic was in his hand. The drawer where it resided was pulled open, sweatpants hanging out.

Cars that drove by, their lights shining through the window displayed a silhouette of two people in death.

Credits rolled up the screen, a classic coming to an end.

Drama Dolls

Emily, her expression unchanged. Staring into the ceiling with her olive colored eyes, alluring as they were. Her shiny black wig of a hair, falling down to the blanket, mixed with a purple red from the blood splatter.

Jeffrey's brain was splashed around the bed. Little bits of human filling the humid room, the stink could be smelled down the hall.

The voice of understanding reason, it was singing to itself.

Jeffrey, ending his agony, he finally joined his wife. He finally joined Her.

And Morrison, he was singing, *"Until the end; Until the end."*

Jason Tanamor

ABOUT THE AUTHOR

Jason Tanamor is the Editor and Founder of Zoiks! Online. Zoiks! Online offers the best in stand-up comedy and music.

He has 10 plus years of experience as an entertainment writer/interviewer for Yahoo!, the Moline Dispatch/Rock Island Argus, Cinema Blend, Celebrity Cafe, Strip Las Vegas Magazine, Pulse Magazine, and Zoiks! Online.

Tanamor has interviewed the likes of author Chuck Palahniuk (Fight Club); comedians Demetri Martin, Jim Breuer (SNL, Half Baked), Aisha Tyler (Talk Soup, The Ghost Whisperer), Dane Cook, and Gabriel Iglesias; musicians Billy Corgan (Smashing Pumpkins), Ann Wilson (Heart), Taylor Momsen (The Pretty Reckless and Gossip Girl), Chad Smith (Red Hot Chili Peppers), and Henry Rollins (Black Flag); and baseball legend Pete Rose.

He has covered everyone from Steve Martin to Jerry Seinfeld and from Evanescence to President Obama.

He also is the author of the critically acclaimed novel, "Anonymous."

Tanamor currently lives in the Portland, Oregon area with his wife and six fur children.

Visit him at www.tanamor.com.

CPSIA information can be obtained
at www.ICGtesting.com
Printed in the USA
FSHW021504020619
58622FS